MW01229075

HILL HOUSE

RECIE D.

Copyright © 2019 RECIE D./P&J PUBLICATIONS

www.RecieDior.com

ISBN: 9798697016053

All rights reserved.

Any unauthorized reprint or use of the material is prohibited. No part of this book may be reproduced or transmitted in any form or by any means, electronic, or mechanical, including photocopying, recording, or by any information storage without express permission by the publisher. This is an original work of fiction. Name, characters, places and incident are either products of the author's imagination or are used fictitiously and any resemblance to actual persons, living or dead is entirely coincidental.

Prologue
May 9th

The blaring car horn rang loudly in my ears, causing me to wake in panic. My eyesight was blurry, and the smell of wet wood and grass filled my nostrils. It didn't take me long to realize I had been in an accident, especially since I was hanging upside down staring out of a cracked windshield. Silence surrounded me. Did I hit something...someone?

Fear rushed through as I tried to move my body. Something was holding me down. Wincing in discomfort, I tried to free myself from the seat belt, but the pain was unbearable. I could feel myself getting weaker and weaker by the moment. And without any hesitation, exhaustion took over.

I closed my eyes.

The feeling of something cold and wet splashed across my face, sending a chill through my body. I opened my eyes and looked around. Panic crawled through my veins. Darkness and rain bounded me.

"Help." I winced, but deep down I knew no one was around to hear me. I strained to get myself free again, but I could not move my right arm. The sound of a snapping twig, followed by a quick scatter, sent a jolt of fear through my body. I wanted to move, but I was frozen.

I tried to stay calm, but anxiety started to set in. I heard a low growl travel over the spattering raindrops. My heartbeat began to quicken as what seemed to be a pair of illuminating blue eyes stared at me in the distance. Clinching my eyelids as tight as I could, I prayed that my mind was playing tricks on me. The hot breath across my face forced my eyes open and before I knew it, I was screaming for my life.

"Help!" I panicked as I tried to get up.

"What's wrong?" I heard a hoarse-like voice call out, before being blinded by light.

It took me a minute to realize that I was not hanging upside down, getting devoured by a wild animal. "Where am I?" I yelled as I tried to look around. "Why can't I move, why can't I see." I continued as panic coasted through my body again. It felt like I was still being held down and something was blocking my peripheral view.

"Spencer, calm down." I heard the voice again and then this short burly light-skinned woman came into view. "You're dreaming again."

"Who is Spencer? Where am I?" I said again, still trying to get up.

"Spencer," the lady said with a low sigh. I stared up at her and watched her alarmed eyes soften. I stopped fighting as things started to become familiar. "Do you remember me?" She asked as she stared hopefully into my eyes. I tried my hardest to remember her, but my mind was drawing a blank.

"Honestly, I can barely remember myself." I replied and I could see the tears forming in my eyes, but whatever was wrapped around my face, stopped them from falling. "What's going on?" I hesitated, not sure if I was ready for her response.

"Spencer, you were in a car accident a few weeks ago. It was really bad; you have a broken arm and leg." She started to say as she looked at my right side. That was the side I couldn't move. "You have burns and lacerations covering your face, the doctors think you might have to undergo a facial reconstructive surgery, if you ever want to look normal again." She explained with a heavy look in her eyes. I sat there in shock, not knowing how to react to her words.

"Am I in the hospital now?"

"No, they released you a few days ago, don't you remember?" Her concerned tone worried me even more.

"No, I-I don't remember anything, it's like my mind is blank." I stammered through the sentence trying to make sense of it all.

"The doctor said that this wasn't going to last long, I didn't know it was going to be this bad." She stopped and took a deep breath. "You had a piece of glass lodged in the back of your head. The paramedics didn't see the glass when they retrieved you. It wasn't until they moved you from the gurney to the hospital bed that they noticed the pool of blood. The glass damaged a part of your brain that controls your memory. You've been waking up in a panic since you've been here." She paused with a quivered lip. I knew whatever she was getting ready to say, was bad news. I could see the nervousness in her eyes.

"What?" I asked, impatiently. The suspense was killing me.

"Every night, you don't remember and every night we have this same conversation. You wake up from a night terror, I run in and you don't remember. We've spent two weeks having this same conversation." She repeated exhaustingly.

"What?" I asked more to myself then her. "I don't understand?"

"It started in the hospital; the doctor let me bring you home a few days ago with the hopes of a familiar place jogging your memory. But it's been three days and you are still waking up without any knowledge of your life."

I stared at her, I wanted to say something, but I didn't know what. I sat back and tried to remember something, anything. But my mind was just a fuzzy mess. Minuscule visions that weren't long enough to get any information from. I couldn't even remember if I knew my name because I remembered it or because she said it. But that wasn't even the scary part, what freaked me out was that this was the fourth night I didn't remember.

I groaned as a sharp pain shot across my head, followed by a queasy feeling growing in my stomach. "This is too much."

"It's ok baby, we are going to get through this. I vowed through sickness and through health." She said as she grabbed my left hand.

It wasn't until then that I realized this woman was my wife. I stared at her plump face and I couldn't help but notice her unattractive features. Her nose was wide, and her eyebrows were bushy. She had tired eyes and big soup cooler lips. It was like she was cute, but in a really ugly way.

"You ok?" She asked, bringing me out of my thoughts.

"Yes, it's just a lot to take in." I admitted, not knowing what else to really say. Seeing her looks made me uneasy about my own.

"Hold on," she said as she stood up and walked out of my vision. I could hear her moving around, but the bandages over my face really limited my view. I wanted to turn my head, but my neck was extremely sore. I just laid still and waited for her to come back into view. I listened to her ramble through some things. "Here we are," she said as she appeared back into view. "Our marriage photo." She continued, while holding up a black frame with an old picture in it.

I grabbed it from her and stared long and hard. Both of us stood lovingly in the picture, smiling as if we had just won a million dollars. Above us was a banner. The names SPENCER AND CELESTE POWELL spread across the front. I stood there. Tall, dark and handsome in my custom tux. Next to me was Celeste. Her slim body, perfect in her fitted wedding dress.

Seeing her now, you wouldn't even recognize her. She was no longer the pretty petite woman in this picture. Her once high yellow vibrant face, was now dry and tired, she had gained a significant amount of weight and a thick, curly, badly cut 'fro replaced her long brown hair. I looked at her and then back to the picture. How could someone so beautiful become so different?

"How long have we've been married?" I questioned, realizing I didn't even know what year it was.

"It will be 19 years, this fall. We got married September 2000."
She replied, as she grabbed the picture and put it back on whatever
she got it from.

"What month are we in now?"

"Today is May 9th, 2019"

"This is too much." I trembled, trying not to cry, but I couldn't
help it. All this information had sent my mind into an emotional
and fearful state. I couldn't move my body. I couldn't remember
anything, and at this point I was a helpless man, stuck at the will of
this woman, my wife.

"I know it is baby, but we will get through it together. I promise."
She replied and placed her hand on my broken leg. I flinched in
pain. "Oh, my goodness, I am sorry. Let me go get your pain
medicine." She said and quickly rushed out of my view again. I
could hear her moving around, but not being able to see was
becoming very frustrating. I closed my eyes and listened to her
talk. "The doctor said these pills are going to affect your dreams,
but your dreams are a form of your memories. We can write down
your dreams every morning and I can help you decipher real from
fantasy." She said as she opened bottles and shook the pills into
something hollow. "Ok here we go," she added as she walked back
into view. "Let me raise your head," She continued and then
somehow cranked the head of the bed up.

"Is this a hospital bed?" I was now sitting up straight and had a better view of her and the room. She shuffled back into my view and I couldn't help but notice something odd about her. She stood with a slump, as if something was weighing her head and shoulders down.

"Something like that," she replied, and I looked at her. I could see her face, but I could barely see her hand or the medicine. I lifted my left hand to reach for it, but I missed it completely. I never realized how much I needed hand and eye coordination until now. "Damn it!" I mumbled in frustration.

"Oh no, we do not use that kind of language in this house Mr. Powell." Celeste chastised me as a look of disgust ran across her face. "Now I know this is a horrible situation but being upset and using vulgar words will not make anything any better. Now open up," she snapped and shoved the pills in my mouth and followed it up with the lukewarm water. It ran down my chin, wetting the bandages as I began to choke. I wasn't expecting her to become so forceful. I guess she could see the shock in my eyes. She suddenly stopped and apologized.

"Oh, my Goodness, Spencer I am so sorry," she said with wide eyes. I must be sleep deprived. Please forgive me," she pleaded while holding my left hand.

"It's ok, I know this has to be a lot for you as well. We are going to get through this." I answered, while giving her hand a reassuring squeeze.

"Oh Spencer, you might not remember, but you always know the right things to say." She smiled and kissed me softly on the lips. "Now get some rest, we will begin your regimen in the morning."

"Regimen?" I asked in a slurred voice, I didn't know what was happening, but I was suddenly extremely drowsy.

"Don't worry baby, it's just the medicine kicking in." Her soothing voice was the last thing I heard before I dosed off.

"Stay with us," I heard a voice call out.

I opened my eyes. Where am I? My mind wandered as my eyes darted back and forth trying to remain focused. I was laying on my back and two people in uniform peered over me. I glanced around at all the medical equipment; I must have been in an ambulance. A sense of relief flowed through my body.

"He's coming too," One of them said as they flashed a light in my eyes. "Hey buddy, do you know your name?" He asked.

My name is…. shoot what is my name. I know I know it. Who am I? My thoughts raced as I tried to remember who I was. I tried to speak, but moving my face stung to bad. Who am I and how did I get here?

"Quick, he's losing too much blood," The other said, jumping into action.

Suddenly my body tensed up and I blacked out again.

When I came too, I was being rushed down a hallway. I could see shadows standing over me. Terror overcame my body when one of the shadows standing over me, eyes started to illuminate a strange blue light.

"Are you ready?" He asked in a sinister voice, followed by the sound of a drill powering up. I watched as he lifted his arm showing me the shiny metal that was rotating at full speed. His blue eyes turned red as he shoved the drill into my legs.

"No!" I yelled as I jumped out of my sleep. Breathing deeply, I tried to calm myself. "It was just a dream." I grumbled as I tried to shift in the bed. The head was still up, leaving me in an uncomfortable position. The room was lighter than it was the last time I woke up, which let me know it was morning. The smell of eggs and bacon filled the air, causing my mouth to water.

I could hear heavy footsteps approaching the door, followed by the sound of the knob turning.

"Good morning honey," Celeste's hoarse voice filled the air as she pushed into the room. She was carrying a bowl and plate. I watched as she moved around the room, coming in and out of my view. I could hear her clumsily shuffling things around as she prepared to serve me. "How are you feeling?" She asked as she pulled out the legs to a serving tray and placed it over me.

"My head is hurting a little bit, but other than that I am ok."

"It might be a hunger headache," she replied. "But I have just the thing for you." She continued with a smile.

"Great, because I am extremely hung-" I started to say but stopped when I noticed the food placed in front of me. "What is this?" I asked in a confused tone, this was not the scent I was smelling in the air.

"Oh, the doctor has you on a strict diet. You must eat certain foods that will help strengthen your bones. So, this morning you have cottage cheese for the protein and the calcium. Orange slices for the vitamin C, whole grain bread for the iron and a handful of nuts for the potassium." She explained, while pointing to each item on the plate.

"Oh," I sighed. I knew she couldn't see my face, but my disappointed tone told it all.

"What's wrong?" She questioned with a raised brow.

"I guess I just thought, it was something else. Because of the smell." I replied while watching her mix the oranges inside of the cottage cheese.

A puzzled look traveled across her face as she sniffed the air. "Oh," she said as she remembered. "Yeah, that was my breakfast." Her light skinned cheeks burned red with embarrassment.

I looked at her and I could tell she was just trying her best to be a good wife. I reached out and rubbed her arm, or what I thought was her arm. She looked at my hand and then back up at me. I tried not to cringe when she scrunched her face up and smiled.

"Oh Spencer," she cheered as she scooped up some cottage cheese in a spoon and brought it up to my mouth. "Open wide." She sang cheerfully.

I instantly wanted to puke as the cottage cheese hit my tongue. The lumpy yet mushy consistency turned my stomach. I tried to swallow it quickly, but it slid down my throat like a slimy snail.

Celeste must have seen the look on my face. She quickly grabbed a cup of water. "I know it's not the best thing," she said as she put the tip of the straw in my mouth. "But it is going to help you get better."

"I know." I said as I finished my sip and opened my mouth for more food. Even though the food was horrible, I knew I needed the nourishment. "So Celeste," I said as I gulped down another scoop. "How did me meet?"

"Oh Spencer, the story is like a fairy tale." Her raspy voice filled with glee as she clutched her hands together. My family and I had come into town to visit my grandmother, the summer right before senior year started. And one sunny day, I was at the beach. I had my feet in the water just minding my business when you came splashing around trying to get my attention. We spent the rest of the day playing and swimming around and just enjoying each other's company." She paused and gazed off in a reminiscing stare.

I sat there with my eyes closed trying to remember, but it was as if my mind was full of static, kind of like a broken television set.

"Oh, after that we were inseparable," Celeste continued with excitement. "We spent the entire summer bowling, going out to eat, holding hands and walking through the park. Oh, my it was just grand." She sighed. "But then the summer came to an end, and it was time for me to leave. We spent one last night together, that was the night you decided to make me a woman." She giggled as if she was back in her school room days gossiping with her girlfriends. "I ran to the house and pleaded to my mother to let us stay, but we had to go back to our hometown."

"So, what happened next?" I asked, completely drawn into the story.

"My grandmother died that night." She said in a sweet yet blunt tone, shocking me for a moment, because it sounded as if she enjoyed saying it. "And in the will, she had left the house to my mother, so I was able to stay." She cheesed as she fed me the rest of the lumpy mixture.

"Wow, it seems like we were meant to be." I paused to take another sip of water. "What was the cause of your grandmother's death, was she sick or something?" I asked in a curious tone.

"No, she slipped and fell over the banister." She replied while turning away from me. "I can still remember the sound of her bones breaking as her body smashed against the floor." She replied in a distant tone. I looked at her and she was once again gazing off and for a moment I thought I saw the corner of her lips forming a smile.

"You ok?" I asked and she quickly turned to me, with tears in her eyes.

"I loved my grandmother." She sniffed, before standing up and walking out of view. "Why would you make me think about her!" She yelled and next thing I knew she was knocking the tray off my lap. The dishes fell to the floor with a loud crash. An eerie vibe came over the room. The sound of the bowl spinning on the floor was the only noise other than Celeste's heavy breathing.

"Celeste, what's going on?" I asked in a nervous tone. I tried to turn my head to see her, but I couldn't.

"Oh, my, what happened?" She said as if she was breaking out of a trance.

"You knocked everything over." I cautioned, trying my hardest not to spark her off again.

"Oh no, I forgot to take my medicine. I am so sorry Spencer." She said as she quickly ran out of the room, leaving me to my own thoughts.

"What the hell?" I said as I shifted my eyes around the room uneasily. I could not get my mind to focus because not only was I on bed rest with limited vision, but I was also married to a damn psycho. "Come on Spencer, remember." I said to myself, while I squeezed my eyes closed, trying to remember something. Anything, about my past. I held my breath as I heard her footsteps approaching again.

"Spencer," her voice was soft and timid. At first, I didn't even recognize it because I was so use to her speaking in a hoarser tone. "I am sorry if I scared you." She paused, walking forward so I could see her better. "I know you don't remember, but I was diagnosed with bi-polar disorder a few months ago and I am still trying to get a hang on it. You were the one who always reminded me to take my medicine, but now," her voice trailed off, but her face was full of emotion.

At that moment, I realized. I might not remember anything, but she does, and she is going through it. Staring into her sunken, tired face, I noticed she was trying to figure it out, just like I was.

"It's ok Celeste, we will get through this together." I said while reaching out my left hand. She glanced at me for a second, before slowly grabbing my hand. "Like you said last night, through sickness and through health." I comforted with an encouraging smile.

"Oh, Spencer." She said with a note of relief.

The relief filled the room and changed the mood completely. I no longer felt scared. And even though I couldn't remember anything, I now understood why I married her. She really loved me. We spent the rest of the day, talking laughing and falling for each other all over again. I know longer saw her as an ugly crazy woman, but as the love of my life, my wife.

June 20th

Fear ran wildly through me as I opened my eyes again. Everything was blurry. I was back in the woods, but I was no longer hanging upside down. I was laying on my back, I could see the night sky above me, and I could feel the wet leaves and bark under me. How did I get here? I asked myself, but before I could find out, I felt a pair of hands grab me underneath my arms. I looked up and was shocked to see a dark hooded figure pulling me. I knew instantly that it had to be death and he was pulling me to my final resting place.

"I'm not ready to die." I said wearily and tried with all my might to pull away from this cold figure. My quick movements worked, causing the figure to let me go. My excitement turned into pain as I fell to the ground and hit my head on a rock.

"Spencer, I am trying to help you." I heard a woman's voice yell out before I blacked out again.

The back of my head throbbed as I laid with my eyes closed. I was still laying on my back, but I was no longer outside on the wet ground. Wherever I was now, it was warm and dry. I tried to open my eyelids, but the light over me was so bright that it almost burned my eyes right out of the sockets.

Turning my head to the side, I caught a glance of three figures standing off in the far-right corner. Their backs were facing me, and they were speaking in hushed tones. I couldn't really hear what they were saying so I closed my eyes and tried to focus more on my sense of hearing.

"Will he live?" I heard a familiar voice.

"It's hard to tell." A male voice replied.

"What do you mean, Charla what does he mean?"

"Celeste your, um, husband has suffered a major head injury. He has a broken arm; a broken leg and he's lost an ample amount of blood. Unless we take him to a hospital," he paused.

"You know I can't do that; I need you to help me. You know, like really help me." Celeste replied in a low panicky tone.

"Celeste are you sure about doing this?" Charla replied.

"Yes, I am sure!" Celeste cried out loud forcing the others to shush her. I quickly closed my eyes and held my breath as I felt them turning towards me. I knew I must have been dreaming, because even though my eyes were closed, I could still see them looking at me. It was as if I was watching a movie starring myself.

I couldn't help but feel a sense of fear in the pit of my stomach. I didn't know what was going on, but none of this felt right. I could hear them talking in hushed tones again. Slowly letting out my breath, I peeked out of my right eye. Relieved to see their backs still to me.

Darting my eyes, I noticed a silver tray sitting on the table next to me. I could see the tip of a knife, and even though I didn't have a lot of strength to fight, I would feel a lot better knowing I had something to protect myself. I looked over to the corner again before I made my move. My right arm was the closes, but I could barely move it. I had to slowly reach over with my left arm without them seeing me.

"Saving Spencer is the only way." Celeste sniffled.

"Spencer isn't," the male voice roared causing me to hit the tray to hard and knock everything over. "Look who's awake," he said, and they all turned towards me. I scrambled to get up, but I couldn't move. "Calm down Mr. Powell," the male voice said as he approached. "We are here to help you. Are you ready?" His voice echoed as his piercing -blue eyes came into view.

He was wearing a doctor's uniform, but I knew this was not a hospital. I tried to fight with my left hand, but he grabbed my wrist and held my arm down. "Rest Mr. Powell." He said and I felt a small pinch in my arm, followed by a cold feeling traveling through my veins. Suddenly my body shook with convulsions, I tried to stop it, but I was out of control.

"Spencer, Spencer!" I heard Celeste's husky voice as she held me down. "Spencer calm down." She continued as my eyes shot open and my body finally stopped shaking. Celeste was sitting next to me on the bed with her hands on my chest. Her worried eyes, searching mines to see if I was still me.

"I'm ok, I'm ok. I was just dreaming." I said with a heavy sigh. It had been a month since the accident, and I didn't understand why I was still having these nightmares. "I didn't mean to scare you." I grunted a little while trying to adjust myself in the bed.

Celeste looked at me strange for a moment and then removed her hand. "Ok," she replied hesitantly, before getting up and starting her morning routine. My vision was still obstructed, but I could hear her.

Every day for the past six weeks, she would come in here, open the blinds and take care of me. I listened to her heavy steps as she moved back and forth through the room. She walked to the bed and cranked up the head. "I thought you said the nightmares had stopped?" She asked as she changed the date on the dry erase board. Her voice was full of concern.

"I thought they did." I mumbled, in a frustrated tone. I hadn't had a nightmare in weeks, and I didn't understand why they were starting back now.

Celeste came back into view and started to set the tray on my lap. "This is the third one since yesterday, what do you think is causing them?" She said while placing the bowl of what smelled like oatmeal in front of me.

"Honestly, I have no clue, but they seem so real." I paused. "In this one, you were dragging me through the woods." I said, causing her to accidently knock over the cup of juice. I shivered as the cold drink spilled over my legs.

"Oh my God," she said as she grabbed the cup and quickly moved the tray. "Through the woods?" She repeated as she pulled the wet blanket off me. I watched her as she moved, if I didn't know any better, I would have sworn she was nervous.

"You good over there babe?"

"Yeah, I'm fine." She paused before changing the subject. "Hey, how about we play a board game today. Doesn't that sound exciting?" She smiled, looking in my direction.

"Yeah, that's fine, but back to this dream." I said and she looked away. "It was crazy, I was laying on a table, but it wasn't a hospital. It was like some type of basement or something. And you were talking to a man and a woman, Charla, I think." I continued and she quickly glanced over at me again. A look of horror dashing across her face. She mumbled something, but I didn't know what.

I began to feel uneasy as the tension in the room grew. "Spencer, I think it's time that you take your medicine." She said in a soft monotoned voice before walking out of view.

"Celeste, what is going on, you are acting really strange." I said as I turned my head slightly to catch a glimpse of her. My stomach dropped when I saw her putting some type of clear liquid inside of a long-needled syringe. "Celeste what are you doing?" I shrieked in fear as she turned around and walked towards me.

"You weren't supposed to remember, something must be wrong." She said in this weird soft voice. I couldn't help but tense up. Hearing her talk like that made my heart race with fear. It was as if she was throwing her voice. "Something must be wrong," she repeated as she came at me with the needle. I didn't know what was going on and I didn't have time to figure it out. I quickly swung my right arm, hitting her in the stomach with my cast.

"Celeste, stop it!" I yelled as I tried to get out on the left side of the bed. I hadn't been on my feet at all, and as soon as I stood up my leg gave out from under me. I screamed in agony as my right arm hit the bedside dresser as I fell. The pain shot through my body as if I had fractured it all over again. I tried to move, but my leg cast was too heavy for my weak body to carry.

"Spencer don't be upset; things are going to work out better next time I promise." Celeste's' slow eerie tone sent chills through my body. The bed springs creaked under her weight. I laid there nervously waiting for her to appear. Something in her eyes told me she was not in her right mind. She slithered down and wrapped herself over me like a snake. I tried to fight, but she had gotten the better hand.

I laid there helplessly as she inserted the needle into my arm. And just like in the dream, an icy feeling traveled through my veins. I fought to keep my eyes open, but it felt as if heavy raindrops were holding them down. My entire body started to go limp. Before I knew it, my mind was shutting down, the last thing I remember seeing was Celeste's oddly smiling face.

I opened my eyes, everything was blurry. My head was pounding, and the spinning of the room was making me nauseated. I heard a hoarse voice talking in the distance. "I don't know what happened?"

"Where am I?" I asked in a panic as I tried to find where the voice was coming from. My vision was blocked, and I began to feel nervous.

"He's woke, I have to go." The person said in a rushed voice before hanging up the phone. "Spencer." I could see a figure slowly coming into view. I was surprised to see that the voice was coming from a woman. "Are you ok?" She continued.

"I don't know, I can't remember anything. Where am I?" I asked, trying to look around the unfamiliar room, but something was stopping my view. "Who are you?" My tone was uneasy as my eyes fell on this stranger's face, I tried to move, but it was as if my body was numb.

"Spencer," she said with a devastated sigh. "You were in a car accident a few weeks ago. It was really bad; you have a broken arm and leg."

"Who are you?" I asked as I tried to search my mind. I didn't recognize her and even though she kept calling me Spencer, I had no idea who that was either. It was as if my entire mind had been erased.

"You had a piece of glass lodge into the back of your head. It damaged a part of your brain that controls your memories." She replied and I sat there stunned.

"Am I still in the hospital?" I asked as I tried to look around the small room.

"No, the doctor let me bring you home. It's been three days and every day you wake up and not remember a thing. The doctor said that it might be from the medicine and you should start remembering again soon." She replied.

"Why can't I see around me?" I said in a panic tone, I could barely handle the information she was giving me, and I was terrified that I had lost some of my eyesight.

"Your face is full of lacerations; the doctor said you might need cosmetic surgery." She replied and I stared at her for a moment. Even though I didn't remember anything, this conversation seemed oddly familiar. It was as if I had heard these words before.

"You said it's been a few weeks, what day is it?" I questioned, still trying to make sense of it all.

"It's May 9th, 2019." She paused and grabbed my left hand. "But don't worry about all that baby, just know that I am here just like I vowed to be. I am here for you through sickness and in health.

Chapter One
July 20th, 2019

Alana Bennett

I laid in the bed, with my head propped up with pillows. In front of me was my laptop and on the screen was numerous of job post. "Secretary...receptionist...daycare worker." I sighed as I read through the list of jobs that I did not want. I didn't really need a job. I just really wanted something that could occupy my time a few hours out of the day, but not have me dealing with a bunch of people. I already got enough social interaction at school.

"Hey little sis?" I heard my brother, Duncan, say as he stood in my doorway knocking on the frame.

"Awwwwe don't you look nice in your uniform." I said admiring his new Sheriff attire. "Over there looking like a damn snitch." I joked and he rolled his eyes.

"Ha, ha, ha." He mocked as he walked in, sat his hat on the dresser and faced the mirror that hung behind him. "Please don't be a hater all of your life."

"Wow, I cannot believe you got the job." I said while sitting up in the bed, I just knew they were going to give it to deputy Jones." I smirked.

"Deputy Jones is almost eighty, the only thing he can sheriff is his breathing machine." He kidded and I couldn't help but laugh.

"So, Sheriff Johnson, what are you going to do when it comes to crime in the city, are you going to show them what the rock is cooking?" I said in my best news anchor voice, while holding out my pretend mic.

He looked at me and cracked a smile and before we knew it, we were both laughing. It felt good to laugh because for just those few moments it made me forget about my heartache. "You are really a nut little sis," he finally said while walking over to the bed. "What you got going on over here?"

"Nothing, just trying to find me a part-time job." I said, looking back at the computer screen.

"Part-time job?" He shrieked with his hand on his chest. "Why are you getting a part-time job, the whole point of me taking this sheriff position was so that you can focus on your studies. What's going on Lani?" His concerned tone irritated me.

"I just need something to occupy my time." I explained with a sigh, even though I knew he was not going to understand.

"School is occupying your time"

"Dunc, I have two summer classes, that end at one. I need something to do for the rest of the day, something that is going to keep my mine of-" I paused letting my voice trail off.

He let out a heavy sigh and put his hand on my shoulder. "Lani," he started to say but I quickly cut him off.

"Please Dunc, I don't wanna get into all of that right now." My tone was full of emotions, one being agitation.

"Listen Lani," he continued trying to comfort me.

"I said I don't wanna talk about it!" I snapped, shocking him. "Damn it Duncan, you aren't mom!" I cried, trying hard to keep the tears from falling.

"I know I'm not Mom, Alana. But before the Alzheimer's took over, she made me promise to look after you and that's a promise I am going to keep." He paused, "Whether your, 'do you smell what the rock is cooking, head ass like it or not." He joked, bringing a smile to my face.

I gave a sigh of relief as the weight in the room lifted. "You a fool bro," I said while shaking my head.

He smirked and then kissed me on the forehead. "Just know I love you girl."

"Alright, now you're pushing it." I laughed while muffing him in the head.

He laughed and then stood up and walked back over to the mirror. "Hey, I'm just trying to get into role. I'm the man of the house now." He mocked, while popping his collar.

"More like the snitch of the city." I joked and he shot me a glance.

"Whatever. Hey," he continued as if he had just got in idea. "How about you come to work at the station. I think there is a receptionist position open." He smiled, while making eye contact with me.

"And be around you all day, forget about it." I said imitating an Italian mobster.

"Aye, stick to your day job. Awe wait that's right you ain't got one." He kidded while doing a quick spin and pointing at me.

All I could do was laugh, "Ha…ha…. Real funny. You better hurry up and get out of here. You know since Covington caught fire; traffic is really slow." I said, noting the stereotype that black folks are always late.

"Yeah you ain't never lied." He said as he grabbed his hat and turned to face me. "Yeah, I make this look good." He said while placing his big sheriff hat on his head.

"You think they ready for a sheriff like you?" I asked, while standing up to get a better look at him. Nodding my head proudly.

He cocked his hat to the side and hit a little gansta lean. "No, the question is, are they ready for a sheriff as fly as me." He said in his best hustler voice and pimp walked out the room. "Catch you later." He added before disappearing down the hall.

"Ight bro, love you." I called behind him before sitting back on the bed and crossing my legs. I couldn't help but be proud of my big brother. Not only was he the new sheriff in town, but he was the first black sheriff this town had seen in years. But like the last sheriff who picked him said, my brother was the right man for the job.

I leaned forward and grabbed my laptop. "Well, let's get back to the search." I encouraged myself while refreshing the page. "Hmmm…what's this?" I said, while noticing a post that was updated seconds ago. "Home aide needed for husband. No certification needed. Must be able to work Monday, Wednesday and some Friday's from 2PM to 8PM but hours can vary. Call number if interested." I read before grabbing my phone.

I pressed the buttons as fast as I could because I did not want anyone else to get it. It was perfect, I only had to deal with one person, the hours are right after school and I don't need any background. This was right up my alley. "Let this be for me Lord," I prayed while anxiously waiting for someone to pick up.

"Hello, Powell residence." I heard a soft and pleasing voice say over the phone.

"Yes, hello. This is Alana Bennett. I came across your Ad and would love to apply for the position." I said in a cheery tone.

"Oh wow, that was fast. I just put the ad up." She replied with a small chuckle. "Either way I am glad you called. Let me tell you about the job."

"Ok."

"So, it is for my husband. He was in a car accident and suffered a few injuries. He has a broken arm as well as a broken leg. His face is covered in lacerations and he is suffering from memory loss." She explained and I instantly felt bad.

"Oh my God. I am so sorry that has happened to you."

"It's ok, it could be worse. We are getting through it one day at a time."

"That's good to hear," I replied with a relieved sigh. I could tell by her voice that she was older, and I knew it had to be hard taking care of her husband by herself. All I could do was picture this little old lady, struggling to lift her man. "So, what would you need help with ma'am?"

"Well, I hope this doesn't come off selfish, but I am in need of some self-care. Taking care of him is starting to affect my health. As well as I don't have time to run errands, because I can't leave him here all alone."

"Oh ok, that's understandable."

"Now, the hours do vary, some days I might get back early and some days I might want to stay out for a bit, but it won't go past eight." She added.

"Ok that is fine. So, what type of things will your husband need help with?" I questioned while reaching into my side table drawer to find a piece of paper and something to write with.

 Well, your duties will include, feeding him meals that I have specially prepared, helping him use the bedpan and then leaving him to his rest." She replied and I tried to write the duties down with the pen, just to find out it was not working.

I shook it with as much force as possible and then scribbled it across the pad, relieved when the ink spread across the paper. "I'm sorry, can you repeat the duties. My phone was breaking up." I lied and listened to her read them off again. "Ok, I got it."

"Awesome. Are you free for an interview today?" She asked, hopefully.

"Um….er…yeah I am." I stammered, a little taken back with her question.

"Awesome. Let me know when you are ready for the address."

"I'm ready now," I said as I thoughtlessly scribbled the words ready now on the page.

"Ok, the address is 1284 Hill street." She replied and I stopped writing.

"You live in the Hill house?" I croaked as the ghost stories about that place circled around in my head.

"Yes, is there a problem?" She inquired.

I quickly gathered my composure, swallowing hard before answering. "Oh no, there is no problem. It is," I paused and looked at the clock. "Going on twelve." I added, knowing it was going to take me about an hour to get there. "How does two sound?" I asked, standing up and rushing to my closet to find something professional looking to wear.

"That's perfect, see you shortly." She replied and we both said our goodbyes.

"The Hill house," I said to myself as I tossed the phone on the bed. "What are the odds that I would pick a job at the creepiest house outside of town. I paused for a moment, doubting my decision, but then I thought about my mother and I knew she would have wanted me to at least go on the interview. She always encouraged me to be the best that I can be and to never let fear cloud my judgement. *You need to stand on your faith.* Her voice echoed in my mind as if she was standing beside me.

I looked at myself in the mirror and all I could see was her. I was 5'3 and curvy just like she was, and my dark chocolate skin tone glistened in the light just as hers did. I was the exact image of her and every way possible. It was that reason why my dad couldn't stand to stay after she got sick. Seeing her in me every day was just too much for him and one morning we woke up and he was gone. Only thing left behind was a note apologizing.

I let out a grieving sigh, before shaking my thoughts away. I just snapped on my brother because I didn't want to talk about it, but here I was thinking on it. "Mom, I am going to make you proud." I said while taking off my clothes and getting ready to make my run for the day.

I couldn't help but stare in awe as the looming appearance of the house came into view. From far it didn't look this big, but up close it was almost threatening. It was an old Victorian style house with two pointed roofs that sat above what looked to be the bedrooms. The panels around the house were a sickly green and the windows were square and needed a new coat of paint

Parking the car, I turned off the engine and let out a deep breath. "Alright Alana, let's make it happen." I said while giving myself and encouraging smile in the rearview. I looked at the house one more time before grabbing my purse and getting out of the car.

"Wow," I hesitated as I came up on the long, narrow and steep steps. There has to be about thirty stairs here. I thought while glancing up. "Well, at least I'll be getting my cardio in." I mumbled as I stepped on the first raised slab of concrete.

Spencer Powell

"Honey," I heard Celeste's groggy voice followed by the shuffle of the curtains. I huffed in my sleep as a ray of sunshine hit my face. "Rise and shine," she continued as she quickly moved around the room. Every day for the past month, she would come in here, open the blinds and take care of me.

"Rise and shine," I grunted as I slowly used my left arm to pull myself up in the bed. I had fell asleep with the head raised and it always left me with a crook in my neck.

"Let me help you," she insisted as she ran over to me.

"I got it," I said in a slightly irritated tone.

"Ok," she startled while moving back.

"I'm sorry." I apologized after seeing the surprised look on her face. "It's just one of those days." I sighed. These last few weeks had been hard on me. I was still bed-ridden because of the cast; my vision was limited because of the bandages and I still couldn't remember who I was.

"It's ok, everything is going to be ok." Celeste assured, but her optimism was starting to get annoying. I watched her smile and walk over to the dry erase board to change the date. I could hear her humming as she moved back towards the window. I couldn't see her anymore, but I could hear the medicine pills rattling in their bottles.

I waited patiently.

Seconds later she came back into view, holding a medicine cup and a bottle of water.

"Here are your morning pain pills and your iron pills." She said while handing me the small plastic up. I quickly tossed them in my mouth and grabbed the bottle of water from her.

The chalkiness of the pills made me squinch, causing a sharp pain to shoot across my face. Celeste assured that it was from my wounds. I'd asked her numerous of times if I could see my face, but her respond was always the same. That the doctor suggested that I don't see my face until it is properly healed.

"Have you talked to the doctor?" I asked while handing the bottle back to her.

"Actually yes, he called in to check on you. "She replied while stepping out of my view again. I hated when she did that because I couldn't see her expressions to know if she was lying or telling the truth. It had been weeks since I've seen or heard from the doctor but let her tell it they are in constant communication.

"Why didn't you let me talk to him?" I asked frustrated.

"Baby, you were sleeping. But I told him about your dreams and I also asked him what would cause you to be healing so slowly." She paused and I could hear her clumsily getting my breakfast together.

"Ok, what did he say?" I asked impatiently.

"Well, he said that one of your medicine's dosage might be too high and he told me what to do to level it out. He said by using less your dreams will stop being so animated and you will start remembering things more clearly." She continued while clearing her throat.

I sat there listening to her talk, but none of this made any sense. *Nothing* made sense. From my injuries, to my memories all the way to the bed sores that were forming on my bottom. It had only been a month, but it felt like I had been in this room for longer. I couldn't put my finger on it, but I knew down in my soul that something weird was going on here.

"What did he say about me healing so slow?"

"It could be because of your age; you are almost forty."

"Forty," I repeated softly to myself. I just did not feel forty, but then again what the hell does forty even feel like.

When she came back in view, she was holding a tray with eggs, a slice of bacon and a smoothie. "Ok, time to eat." She sang, cheerfully. I tried to look down as she sat the tray on my legs, but the bandages once again obstructed my view. My helplessness turning into frustration as she began to feed me.

"Why do you continue to deal with me, I know you are tired of taking care of me." I muttered.

"Why would you say that, I am your wife and I vowed to be here through sickness and in health." She expressed with lifted eyebrows. I rolled my eyes; it was as if I had heard her say that a thousand times. Sometimes it would feel like Déjà vu.

She stuffed a spoonful of eggs into my mouth as I continued to stare quietly. There was just something off about her, I could see it in her eyes I just didn't know what it was. I blinked a few times and looked away. I hated having these thoughts about her, especially since she's been taking such good care of me, but I wish I just knew more about her. My mind drifted off as I slowly chewed the food. Visions of our wedding started to show. I couldn't remember the actual wedding at all, but I had created my own version of it from the pictures I've seen and the stories she told me.

I wish she still looked the way she did in the pictures, it would probably make this situation a whole lot better. "How long have we've been married again?" I asked after swallowing. I knew I knew the answer, but lately I had started to forget my current memories as well.

"It will be ten years, this fall." She stated while putting the smoothie to my lips. "Remember we got married September 2000." She replied and I wanted to smack her.

"No, I don't remember." I yelled, banging my left hand on the table causing the juice to spill. The cold liquid falling on my legs felt strangely familiar. I couldn't help but think that all of this had happened before. She quickly apologized and I instantly felt bad after seeing the surprised look on her face. "No, I'm sorry." I said calmly. "You are just trying to help me." I paused. Suddenly a wave of emotions came over my entire body and I had to literally keep myself from crying. "It's just hard not being able to remember anything." I wailed, finally letting the tears flow.

I felt weak and helpless as she cleaned up the mess I made. I didn't know what was going on with me, it was like I was splitting into two different people: the person I was before the accident and the person I am now. I just wish I had a better understanding on what was happening to me. I'm at the point where I am remembering things that doesn't seem to fit in this life I had with Celeste. I've been seeing a woman in my dreams and even though I can never see her face. I knew it wasn't Celeste.

I told her about the dream a few nights ago and she got really upset. She yelled at me for not being appreciative enough and told me that I was selfish and that I had always been. She cried the rest of the day and I felt so bad. I think I had dreamed of an affair that I don't remember having. After that I stop telling her my dreams, she was already dealing with so much. Between me, her disorder and my not so good memories I could tell she was holding on for dear life.

"I'm sorry," I said, and she looked up at me. Her eyes were tired, and her smile was sad. It was at that moment, I realized that maybe the reason she looks the way she does now is because I caused her so much pain in the past.

"It's fine Spencer!" She said in an angered tone. "No, you know what! Everything is not fine. I just washed these sheets from the last juice spill!" She blurted while scrubbing the sheets together as if that was going to get the juice out.

I tensed up as I noticed she was going into one of her episodes. "Baby, did you take your medicine?" I asked politely.

"No, I didn't take it because I am too busy taking care of your whiny ass. Oh, woe is me, I am Spencer and I get to lie in bed all day while my wife slaves." She screamed, causing me to brace myself. Celeste hated foul language, so when I heard her curse. I knew what was coming next.

"Owwwww Celeste," I screamed in pain as she pounded her fist on my casted leg. "Baby you have to calm down," I said in pain. "Breathe, Celeste breathe." I repeated while breathing in and out slowly. I watched as her deranged eyes started to simmer as she exhaled with me. "There you go baby, now go take your medicine." I said and she turned and walked out of the room as if she was a lifeless puppet being controlled by strings.

When she was out of earshot, I closed my eyes and let out a deep breath. Being confined to this bed was terrifying. I never know when Celeste was going to go off her rocker. One day I woke up and she was standing over me with a knife, telling me to get out of her husbands' body. She claims that it was one of my nightmares, but I am for sure that it was not.

I was startled when I opened my eyes again. Celeste was standing oddly in the doorway. When did she get there? I didn't hear her footsteps, which was strange because she walks extremely heavy. "Hey babe, are you ok now?" I asked hesitantly.

"Why yes, I am." Her voice was soft and distant as she moved closer into the room. I noticed that she wasn't slumped over like usual. She was standing straight and poise. "Hun, can I ask you a question?" She continued.

"Um, sure." I cautioned as I slowly started to adjust myself in the bed. She was standing with her held tilted to the side and her arms behind her back. There was this look in her eyes as if she was not herself, and I couldn't help but feel that I had seen it before. The hairs on my arms started to stand as this familiar feeling of uneasiness came creeping across my body. She continued towards me. Her eyes focused on mine as she slowly moved to the left side of the bed, which was awkward because she never stands on this side of me.

"How did the juice waste all over the bed?" Her tone was pleasant as she continued to walk towards me. The question confused me more than I thought it would. She had knocked over the juice when I told her my dream. Or did I knock over the juice. I sat quiet as these two memories crossed over into each other and I started to realize what was happening.

"Um, you did, remember?" I hesitated as I looked up at her. Every part of me hoped she would take my answer and move on. I smiled at her; I didn't want her to know that I was remembering.

"You know Spencer," She said as she softly caressed my arm. "I can always tell when you are starting to remember. You get this focused look on your face and it is a dead giveaway." She paused and grabbed my arm tightly. "Why can't you just let us be happy?" She yelled and before I could do anything else, she shoved a needle into my arm

"Celeste," I wept as the icy feeling rushed my veins. Confusion filled my mind as I stared at her twisted face. I could feel myself fading into darkness, the last thing I seen was Celeste staring down at me, smiling strangely.

Celeste Powell

I stood over Spencer's body and watched his panic eyes drift. Once he was out, I put the needled down and started to straighten up the room, making sure everything was strategically placed as it was before he started to remember. I glanced around the room, one last time before turning off the light and making my exit.

I crossed the hall and walked into my bedroom, slamming the door behind me. Why was this not working? I wondered as I threw the empty syringe on the dresser next to the glass medicine bottles. I had seen the doctors use this medicine on many people and it always worked.

I don't know what it is about that man, but his mind just will not let him forget. I've upped the dose twice, but still he remembers, and I can't have him remembering.

Grabbing a pillow off the bed. I placed it over my face and let out the loudest scream. All I wanted was to be happily married, but if these memories continue to manifest in his mind. It could be detrimental for not just me, but for my friends. "Why can't he just forget the past and accept the present." I mumbled as I threw the pillow across the room.

The clinking sounds of glass broke the silence as the pillow landed on the dresser. "No," I shouted as I ran over to the mess, making sure the bottles had not broken. I didn't have much of the medicine left, which was odd. I was only giving it to Spencer, right? I questioned myself as my mind continued to wander.

I stood in front of the mirror, catching a glance of myself. I noticed how drained my stress filled face looked. At one point I had everything under control. I was taking my medicine; I wasn't stress and I felt like I could live with this diagnosis. But now, with everything happening with Spencer, I can feel myself slowly losing the battle. I needed a break, but the way things were looking, I was never going to get one.

Thinking about this situation was starting to give me an anxious sensation. The feeling was coming a lot more lately, and if I failed to catch it, I would find myself having an outer body experience. I took a deep breath as my mind traveled back a few nights. I was standing over Spencer with a knife and I don't even remember getting out of my bed. It was like someone had taken control of my body while I slept.

"Breathe," I grunted to myself as my right hand began to shake. I grabbed it with my left and tried to keep myself from falling apart. I quickly searched the dresser until my eyes fell upon my anxiety medicine. I could feel the beads of sweat sliding down my face and I knew if I didn't get a grip now, I was going to end up doing something crazy.

Taking another deep breath, I reached out and tried to grab the pill bottle, but I ended up knocking over a picture instead. In that moment, I could feel myself getting distracted. I stared purposelessly at the picture and admired the beautiful woman staring back at me. I looked at my reflection and then back at the picture. I hadn't seen that woman in weeks, when did I replace her.

I could feel my body getting inpatient and, in that moment, it felt as if I was being watched. I slightly looked up at my reflection, but the person in the mirror was already staring at me. I put my hand over my mouth and muffled a scream, but she didn't move. She just stared at me with a twisted smile on her face.

"This is not real," I shuddered. Closing my eyes, I repeated the mantra over again. "This is not real." I yelled as I opened my eyes again. My reflection stood there, smiling. Suddenly a syringe appeared in her hand. I watched in fear as she moved closer and held it over her right arm. I looked in my right hand and I was still holding the medicine bottle. I looked at her again and then quickly tried to open the top, but she was faster than me. Icy fear ran through my body, forcing me to drop the pill bottle. I fell to my knees in pain, it was too late, no number of pills could help me now. My reflection had taken over and I could feel myself growing powerless as a state of darkness grew over me.

The doorbell rang, startling me out of a hazy sleep. "How did I get down here?" I wondered, while glancing around the living room. I stood up quickly still puzzled. "What the-" I started to say but was cut off by the doorbell ringing again. Who is at the door this early in the morning? I thought as I rushed to the door and grabbed the knob.

My eyes widened as the door swung open. I was shocked to see this young, bright eyed curvy woman standing in front of me. I raised my brow in confusion as I peeked around her.

"Yes, may I help you?" I asked, realizing she was alone.

"Hi, I'm Alana Bennet, I am here to see Mrs. Powell."

"I am Mrs. Powell." I replied indecisively, as I stared at this pretty *young* woman. It was something really familiar about her, but I couldn't quite put my finger on it.

"Oh, Mrs. Powell, your voice sounded so different when we talked on the phone earlier." She replied, and I stared silently at her. She must have noticed the bewildered look on my face because she quickly pulled out her phone to show me something. "You posted this ad earlier, saying you needed a care giver. Now I know I look young, but I am twenty-three, a people person and I am also a hard worker." She explained and I read over the ad, shocked to see that I had posted it around eleven.

It was now two-something and the last thing I remembered was giving Spencer his breakfast. I didn't understand why I couldn't remember these last six hours.

"Mrs. Powell are you ok?" Alana's worried voice pulled me out of my thoughts.

"Oh yes, I am so sorry." I said as I moved back to let her into the house. The smell of her sweet perfume hit my nose as she brushed by. I closed the door and turned to her.

"Wow, this is a big house." She said in awe as she glanced around, looking from the ceilings down.

"Oh yes, it is very roomy," I replied as I admired her beauty. Wondering where could I get a glow like hers.

"So, is there anything you would like to know about me?" She asked, pulling me out of my thoughts.

"Yes, I am sorry. I am completely out of it. You are here for an interview, so let's get it started." I replied, still not knowing what was going on, but I didn't want to miss this opportunity to get some social interaction. "Wait in the living room, I have some lemonade and cookies. I'll bring them out." I continued and motioned her to sit down before I disappeared into the kitchen.

I couldn't believe my eyes, when I walked in and saw the computer sitting on the table. I walked over to it and there was the ad, clear as day. Maybe it was Spencer? The thought ran across my mind, but at this point, I knew I must have been losing it. I could not remember even working on the computer today at all. I quickly scanned through the ad, grabbed the refreshments out of the refrigerator and appeared back out front.

"Oh, do you need any help," Alana said as she jumped up and grabbed the tray, carefully placing it on the table before plopping back down on the couch.

"Thank you, you are such a sweet girl." I replied as I sat across from her and started to pour the glasses of lemonade. "I see why you answered the ad, you must enjoy helping people?"

"Yes, I do enjoy helping people. My mother always said it is better to give than to receive. I don't have much to give, so I give my time." She replied while grabbing the glass and taking a sip. "Wow, this is very good. Did you make it yourself?" She continued while taking another sip.

"Not really, it's one of those pre-made powders, the one you add water to." I said with an embarrassed laugh.

She leaned forward, "Don't worry." She whispered, "Your secret is safe with me." She continued with a smile and I smiled back.

"You know what Alana; you have the job." I blurted without notice, shocking us both. "I mean," I continued with a nervous laugh. "I like your personality and I think you would be a nice help around here." I finished with a big smile. I couldn't help but feel some type of excitement with her being here. I had been alone for so long and I couldn't help but imagine all the fun things we could do together.

"Awesome," She cheered while clapping her hands together. "So, will I be able to meet your husband today or should we just wait until Monday when I start." She replied, bringing my happiness from a ten all the way down to a one. I was so busy fantasizing about having a some-what daughter that I forgot the reason she was here.

"Oh, honey," I said in a soft voice. "You will meet him Monday. I want to give him time to agree as well as let you know more about his condition." I said and let out a heavy sigh. "Spencer is getting worse. He spends weeks healing and then out of the blue he forgets everything all over again. The doctors do not know what is causing his diagnosis. They think his brain is so damaged that it restarts all on its own." I explained and watched as the sorrow spread across her face.

"Oh my, I am so sorry."

"Don't be, it's not your fault. But I just want you to know what to expect. He could remember you one day and the next day he could be saying it's May. For some reason that is the month he always goes back to. I've learned to just go with the flow, as I would appreciate if you would as well." I continued giving her a stern look.

"Oh yes, absolutely." She replied and I smiled.

"Great, oh and he tends to have these very vivid dreams and it is very important that if he tell you these dreams you let me know as soon as possible. They can sometimes be a sign of his relapse. I will have a regimen written up by Monday" I paused. "Do you have any questions?"

"No, I will wait until I see what you write up." She answered and I nodded.

"Well Ms. Bennet..." I started but was cut off by Spencer screaming upstairs. "Oh no, he is having one of his nightmares again. Alana, I have to attend to him, will you be able to let yourself out?" I said hoarsely, halfway up the stairs.

"Yes, no problem." I barely heard her say as I ran into the room to comfort Spencer. I could feel myself getting frustrated as I looked into his clueless eyes. His mind had started all over again.

July 22nd

Alana

"Hey bro," I said as I rushed past Dunc and headed up to my room, grabbed my cell phone charger and then hopped down the stairs. "Today is my first day and I do not want to be late." I said trying to push pass him.

"Hold on," he said grabbing my arm. "Lani, I really do not like the fact that you have to make that long drive and work up there at that house. The place does not have a great reputation." He said in a worried tone.

"Now I know Sheriff Johnson does not believe in ghost stories." I joked, while wiggling my fingers at him.

"No, I just want to make sure you are safe. If something was to happen while you were out there, I would not be able to get to you quickly." He explained.

"I understand bro, but Mrs. Powell is cool, and her husband is bed bound. What is the worst that could happen?" I asked and waited impatiently for a response. "Exactly," I said before he could give me an answer.

"Why can't you just work full time at the station?" He whined.

"Because two days is already more than enough time I want to spend with you." I kidded, before giving him a kiss on the cheek.

"Love you bro, don't wait up." I said before skipping out of the house and making my trip up the hill.

I pulled up to the house at exactly two. Grabbing my bookbag, I quickly hopped out the car, sprinted up the stairs and rang the bell. "Sorry I'm late," I said as Celeste opened the door.

"Oh honey," her voice was scratchy as if she had a cold. "You don't have to worry about being here at exactly two. I know you said you were in school." She continued as she walked me into the house. "Ok, as you know My husband, Spencer, was in a bad accident. He's bed ridden and sometimes needs help getting on the bed pan." She described while pulling out a folded piece of notebook paper and handing it to me. "I have him on a strict diet, so when he gets hungry just pull out one of the pre-made meals in the refrigerator. It's also extra food marked for you, if you get hungry as well." She paused and looked around. "Let me give you a quick tour," She added while leading me through the house. "Of course, this is the front room and there is a bathroom around this corner." She said while pointing.

"Ok," I noted as we continued into the kitchen. "What is this, a pantry?" I asked, while glancing at the big wooden door that sat next to the stove.

"No, this door leads to the basement, but it is off limits." She said in a soft voice. It was the voice that I remembered when I first talked to her on the phone. The way her voice changed kind of creeped me out. If I would have had my eyes closed, I would have thought it was another person in here with us.

"Ok," I replied, brushing off my weird feeling.

"There is a bunch of mold spores down there and I don't want anyone to get sick." She added, while pulling at the knob. "I keep it locked."

"Ok," I replied, and we headed back into the front. "Is this your husband?" I asked while picking up a picture of a tall man holding a bowling ball.

"Yes, that is Spencer." She said lovingly, while removing the picture from my hand. "He was such a handsome man." She said, staring at the picture, before setting it back on the table.

"Was?" I asked hesitantly.

"I mean," she started with a panic look on her face. "He is still handsome. His face is just badly bruised right now." She reminded me and I instantly felt dumb.

"Oh, right. I'm sorry Celeste." I replied and she smiled.

"Don't be honey," she replied as we walked towards the stairs. "Because of his hospital bed, we do not share the same room. His bedroom was once the guest room. Now because of his accident his face must always be covered. Don't worry about changing the bandages because I do that every morning and every evening. He's in the healing process so let him rest as much as possible." She added as we walked up the stairs. She stopped in front of the room and turned to me. "The day you left his memory relapsed. So, we are back to square one." She whispered to me before knocking on the door. "Spencer," she called out. "I have someone I want you to meet."

I could barely hold my composure as Spencer's body came into view. "Oh," I mumbled before walking into the room.

"Spencer this is Alana, she is going to be your caregiver on days where I need to run errands." She replied introducing us.

"Hello Alana," his weak voice called out from behind the bandages. I wanted to reply but I was loss for words. This man looked at if he was days away from death. His body was frail, and the bandages and cast made him look like a mummy. His bed was in the up position, but he could barely keep himself straight.

"Hi Spencer," I said in a cheery tone, trying my best not to sound frightened.

"Baby, I am going to run out for a few hours. If there is anything you need, don't hesitate to call Alana. She is here to help you." Celeste replied, but Spencer just closed his eyes and ignored her. "We will let you get your sleep." She said and we both walked out of the room. "Sorry you had to see him like that. He hasn't been eating lately.

"Don't apologize, I know you are doing your best." I comforted, bringing a smile to her face.

"You are definitely going to lift the spirits in this old house." Celeste responded as we walked down the stairs. I watched as she checked her watch. "Oh my," she said in a shocked tone. "I have to get going if I want to catch some sales. I'll be back around seven." She continued while grabbing her bag and heading towards the door. "All my numbers are on the refrigerator, call me if you need anything." She paused, and then quickly turned to me. "Please remember to not remove his bandages under any circumstances. His face is very sensitive and it's a certain way that it needs to be handled. Do you understand?" She asked in a stern yet tenderly tone.

"Yes ma'am," I replied.

"Ok, have a great day," was the last thing Celeste said before the door closed behind her.

Spencer

I opened my eyes as I heard Celeste and another pair of footsteps come up the stairs. I wanted to fix myself up in the bed, but my body was weak. The last couple of days I had been fighting a terrible headache and I couldn't keep anything down. All I wanted to do was sleep the pain away.

I heard a knock on the door followed by Celeste voice. "Spencer, I have someone I want you to meet." She said and then opened the door, unveiling this beautiful, chocolate curvy woman. "Spencer this is Alana, she is going to be your caregiver on days where I need to run errands."

Hello Alana," I croaked, wishing I had at least sat up in the bed a little. I probably looked like some type of corpse laying here. Celeste said something to me, but I was so embarrassed all I could do was just close my eyes and pretend to be sleep.

I opened my eyes again and listened as Celeste reminded Alana not to remove my bandages, her tone was stern as if she was a mother talking to her child. Alana must have felt the same way because she replied with yes ma'am. I heard the door open and close and the house fell silent.

For a moment I thought Alana left out, but then I heard her soft footsteps as she crossed the room. "He's resting, so I guess I'll get some work done." She said to herself and then I heard a few shuffled sounds, a thud and pages flipping. It was amazing how sharp my senses had become since the accident.

"Now if only I could get my mind to act right." I huffed while closing my eyes and laying back into the bed.

"Where am I?" I asked as I looked around, surprised to see that I was sitting in the backseat of a car. There was a woman driving in

the front. "Where are we going?" I asked but she didn't respond. I tried to open the doors, but the sight of seeing my hand without a case over it stunned me. I tried to catch a glance of my face, but the image was blurred. "Who am I?" I asked, but when I looked at the driver she had disappeared.

The car began to speed as I tried to get into the front seat, but no matter how hard I tried I could not move. When I looked down again my entire right leg had disappeared, followed by my arm. I yelled for help as the car continued to speed towards a busy intersection.

"Help, Help!"

"Help me," I screamed while waking up from the dream.

"Are you ok?" Alana panicked as she burst into the room.

I-I was having a bad dream." I panted heavily. "What time is it?"

"It's going on five-thirty." She replied with her hand on her chest, panting to catch her breath.

"Sorry, I didn't mean to scare you. I've been having nightmares. The doctor said it's a way of my mind trying to remember." I explained.

"It's ok, as long as you are ok." She replied and started to turn to the door.

"Where are you going?" I asked not wanting to be stuck in this room alone any longer.

"Oh, on the schedule Celeste left me, it says to heat up your meal when you wake."

"No that's ok, I'm not hungry right now." I said, even though my stomach was growling from under the covers. Maybe it was my ego, but I didn't want to seem helpless to this fine ass woman. And what's more helpless then having to be fed. Plus, I figure if I don't eat, I won't have to go to the bathroom until Celeste gets here. I can't have this woman wipe my ass, that's just unheard off.

"Oh, ok." She said and we both just stared awkwardly at each other. I could feel myself getting nervous, but I didn't understand why. "Well, do you want some company?" She asked with a smile.

"Actually yeah, I do." I replied and she walked over to the recliner that sat in the corner. "You are going to have to pull it over, you are now out of my view." I said while pointing to the bandages on my face.

"Oh, I'm sorry." She giggled nervously before standing up and pulling the recliner closer. "Is this better?" She asked with her back to me.

"Yeah, that's better." I said admiring the view. I wasn't trying to be a pervert. It was just nice looking at something other than Celeste and her badly built body.

"Are you ok?" She asked trying to start conversation.

"Yeah, I'm fine." I said as I tried to adjust myself in the bed.

"Let me help-" She started to say but I cut her off.

"No, I need to do this on my own." I replied. "If I don't use my own muscles, I will lose them."

"How is your physical therapy going?" She questioned with raised brows.

"Physical therapy?" I asked and realized maybe she didn't know that I was just recovering. "Oh, I haven't started it yet. It's only been a few weeks and I've only been home for maybe three days." I continued.

"Oh, right." She said, with her face quickly changing from confused to normal. "I'm sorry, I forgot."

"It's ok, I forget a lot to." I said while pointing to my head. Her face flushed with embarrassment. I quickly smiled to let her know I was just joking.

"Oh, you got me." She said, with a hesitant laugh. "So," she paused, and I could tell she was thinking. "You really don't remember anything, like nothing at all?"

"I mean," I paused, trying to get my thoughts in order. "I am starting to remember, but not really." I replied and I could see her face ready for an explanation. I couldn't help smiling at the way it was scrunched. She looked like a cute little bunny rabbit.

"What?" She asked in a soft tone.

"Nothing," I replied in a tone so smooth, I could see the lust sparkling in her eyes. Hell, I might not remember a lot, but you never forget how to be a player. I laughed at the thought, before finally answering. "But to explain, my memories are somewhat there, but they are distorted."

"What do you mean by distorted?" She asked, curiously.

"When I see pictures or if Celeste tells me a story about how we met, or our wedding. I make those memories of what I think happen myself. But when I try to remember anything from my past, I get like a static picture and sound." I paused. "If that makes any sense."

"Yeah, it actually makes perfect sense. Especially with your injuries. The part of the brain that stores those memories is damaged. It will take some time, but those memories will come back."

"How do you know?" I asked curiously.

"I am actually going to school for psychology and we spend a lot of time studying the brain." She replied and I was instantly in awe.

"Beauty and brains." I flirted and she smiled. I don't know what it was, but it felt good to have someone, other than Celeste here to just talk to. A part of me felt kind of bad, feeling that way. But with Alana, I didn't even have to try and remember things because this was all new. And it didn't help that she was finer than a glass of wine at dinner time. "What made you want to get into that field?"

Well, my mother developed a strong case of Alzheimer's in the beginning of May. Her diagnosis has gotten so bad that she can't remember anything. It came on so sudden and the doctors don't know how.

"The beginning of May," I said as I looked at the date on the board. "So it's only been about a week. How are you able to function?"

"Oh." She paused as her eyes glanced at the date as well. "Yeah, about a week. I took the job to keep my mind off of things." She replied in a nervous tone.

"Oh yeah, I can understand that. I'm sorry that you have to work with someone that has also lost their memories. I know that has to be hard." I said, referring to myself.

"It's ok. I can handle it."

I watched as she twisted back and forth, looking around the room. It seemed as if she was trying to avoid making eye contact with me. "How suddenly did it come?"

"Excuse me?" She said as she stopped moving.

"You said her Alzheimer's came so sudden. How sudden was it?"

"Oh yeah. Well," she paused as if she was thinking of the right words to explain. My mother worked at the Covington Asylum that's just outside of town. The night she lost her memories there was a riot and some of the inmates got lose. When they found her, she was laying on the floor, bleeding from her head. Whoever hit her, hit her with so much force that her memories just faded." She explained with tears in her eyes.

"Damn, I'm sorry," I said with tears in my eyes as well. I felt bad because I was going through the same thing with my memories and I wouldn't wish that on my worst enemy.

"So, for me and my brother, it was suddenly. She left the house knowing who we were and the next time I seen her half of her memories were gone.

"It's been hard, but I'm getting through it." She sniffed, and I wished I could just go over there and comfort her. "But," she started to say while wiping her eyes. "The abruptness of it made me curious, so I took it upon myself to learn everything about the disease. I didn't know I was going to love learning about the brain and how our mind works so much." She paused to take a breath. "So yeah, it makes sense that you are not remembering anything if a certain spot was injured in the accident."

I was getting ready to say something, but a sudden feeling of light headedness fell upon me and my head fell back into the pillow.

"Oh no, are you ok?" She said and I couldn't help but notice her huge breast jiggling as she rose out of the seat.

"Yeah, I'm ok, don't get up." I replied and she slowly sat back in the chair.

"Are you tired, do you want me to go?"

"No," I shouted startling her a bit. "I mean no," I said calmly. "It's just really nice to have someone to talk to that isn't expecting me to be someone else."

"Someone else?" She asked with a curious brow.

"Yeah, the Spencer before the accident. Celeste is waiting for him to come back, but right now I am not him. Hell, I am not sure who I am." I laughed, trying to lighten the mood. She smiled and gave me an understanding head nod before resting back into the recliner.

We sat quiet for a while, both of us in our own thoughts. My mind wandered back to the last few days. Sitting here meeting Celeste for the first time and hearing her tell me about how we met, all seemed like Déjà vu. Even though I don't remember anything, it is some things that she does and say that seems oddly familiar.

"So why are you not eating?" Alana asked, breaking the silence.

"I am just tired of eating baby food." I said, letting out a disappointed sigh.

"She's feeding you baby food?" She shrieked loudly and then put her hand over her mouth to contain her astonishment.

I laughed and shook my head. "No, it's not like foreal baby food, but she feeds me cottage cheese, fruits and nuts like I am some type of rabbit or something. I am a grown ass man and I need a grown ass meal. Look at me, it looks like I ain't ate in months, I am skin and bones." I said in a raised voice, startling her. "I'm sorry," I continued as I calmed my nerves.

"It's ok, I understand you are frustrated." She replied in a heavy tone.

"Frustrating ain't even the word. I just wish I were better. I think once I get my mind right, my body will follow."

"How about on the days I am here, I help you do some memory exercises?" She suggested.

"Oh my God, why haven't I thought about doing memory exercises. Wait, what are memory exercises?" I said, realizing that I had no clue what she was talking about.

"Memory exercises are different tools that can sharpen the brain's ability to record information and helps create a clearer memory. They can also help with your recall." She replied as if she was reciting from a textbook. She must have noticed the look on my face because she followed her statement with, "I literally just read it in my psychology book before I came up here."

"So, what are the tools, am I going to have to by a machine or something?"

"No, not really. Hold on," she said as she quickly jumped up and left out of the room. I listened as she ran down the stairs, shuffled through some things and then quickly shot back up the stairs. I couldn't help but envy her mobility. "Ok," she panted as she stepped back into view, this time holding a baby blue bookbag. I watched as she dropped it on the floor, grabbed out a thick textbook and flipped through the pages. Her face lit up as she landed on the right one. "Ah ha, here it is."

"What, what does it say?" I asked anxiously.

"Ok, it says," she paused and scrolled the page with her finger. "Here are a few things you can do to sharpen your mental skills. Make a list, such as a grocery list and memorize it. In an hour see how much of the list you can recall. Another thing you can do is start journaling."

"Journaling," I sneered cutting her off. "What am I, a high school girl?"

"Spencer, journaling is a great way to express things to yourself, especially your dreams. You can write them down and go back and review them. Or you can write about different things that are happening in the day, and for those times where you forget. You can go back and reread it. I know it sounds crazy, but no one has to know you are doing it, this is just some stuff you can do for yourself." Her voice was cheerful, and I couldn't help but give in.

"Ok, your right," I huffed. "What else does the book say. Am I going to have to get my hair and nails done to?" I joked.

"Well, it wouldn't hurt." She joked back and we both started laughing. "And I'll get you some word search and crossword puzzles. Those help a lot with memory as well." She continued as she pulled out a notebook and pen from her book bag. After quickly jotting something down, she ripped out the page, stuck it in her book bag and closed the notebook. "You can have this; it is practically new." She said, while standing and handing me the book and pen.

"I don't even know how I will write in this book; I can't see it; I can't hold it up and hell I don't even know if I am right or left-handed." I complained and instantly I could see the color drain from her face.

"Oh right, damn it I am so stupid. I'm sorry Spenc," she said while plopping down in the chair. A look of defeat plastered on her pretty round face.

"It's ok Shorty, we'll think of something else." I replied in a softer tone, disappointed with myself for breaking her spirits.

"Shorty?" She asked in an animated tone. "Where you from, Brooklyn or something?" She kidded, while doing her best New York accent.

I couldn't help but shake my head and laugh. It really felt good to have her here. I don't think I've smiled this much since I woke up. Celeste is either always to serious or to pleasant, there isn't really an in-between. And she never talks to me about anything real, she spends majority of the time analyzing me as if she's waiting for me to turn into a pumpkin or something. It's annoying and sometimes I feel like I am a prisoner in my own home. Laying in this room day in and day out, nothing knew happening. Alana being here is definitely what I needed; it just lets me know that I gotta get myself together. It is an entire world out there that I am missing out on.

I sat back in the bed as the room fell silent for a bit, both of us were lost in our own thoughts. I was about to spark up another conversation, but her phone rang.

She grabbed it and then stood up. "Give me a second." She said and quickly rushed out of the room, pulling the door slightly closed. "Hey…yeah I am at work…no I didn't leave the door open. Ugh, Duncan I am at work. Yeah, I'll talk to you later." She replied and then walked back into the room.

"Who was that, your boyfriend?" I snooped and she laughed.

"Boyfriend, ha. I don't have time for one of those. No that was my big brother." She said, still standing by the door. The room went silent again but was suddenly filled with the growling of my stomach. "Oh, let me get your food."

"No, I'm ok." I replied and she looked at me strange.

"Oh, I see." She said realizing my issue. "I got something for you." She continued and then quickly left out of the room.

I sat there for a few minutes still enjoying the smell of her lingering perfume. I could hear her downstairs heating up whatever jail food Celeste had left for me. Celeste was a good woman, but Lord knows she could not cook worth a damn. I heard the microwave end and a few minutes later I could hear Alana coming up the stairs.

"Ok," she said as she walked in the room with the bed tray full of magazines. She sat it at the foot of the bed and then went back to retrieve the food. I couldn't help but wonder what she was doing as she set up the tray and the magazines in front of me, but when she sat the food on top it all made sense. "Can you see the food?" She asked.

"Yeah, I can." I replied as I looked in the divided Tupperware bowl and frowned. "But now I wish I couldn't."

"Don't be like that, I am sure it is going to be good!" She exclaimed as she put a fork in my left hand. "Now, I have no clue what it is, but this is what she had marked for today." She said and I laughed. I loved her optimism.

"Man, I don't even care what it is, I am just happy to be able to feed myself." I replied, stuffing a forkful of what I assumed was liver and onions into my mouth. I instantly regretted it once the bland taste hit my tongue. I was about to push it away, but another scent hit my nose. I looked up and watched as Alana unwrapped her plate of food. "Damn, what you got?" I asked in a jealous tone.

"Oh, nothing. Just some fried chicken, baked macaroni, homemade mashed potatoes, greens and some cornbread that I cooked yesterday." She replied nonchalantly.

"And you ain't got a man?" I asked while trying to catch the dribble of slob that was escaping my mouth.

"Ain't got time for one." She replied and then took a bite of her crispy chicken wing. I watched with my mouth open as she enjoyed each bite. I wanted to cry as I looked from her meal to mine.

"Girl come on and let me get some of that good food. You see me over here eating this plate of horse shit." I replied, pushing the bowl of mess out of my sight.

"No, Celeste said she has you on a strict diet, I do not want to go against her order." She replied while licking her fingers.

"Listen, I've been laying in this same spot for I don't even know how long anymore, eating this crap," I whined while pointing to the bowl of mush. A little bit of chicken is not gonna hurt me."

"I don't want to get in trouble Spencer, I need this job." She said as a worried look overtook her face.

"Listen, I promise that any and everything that we do in this room will never be discussed. I'll even eat a little of whatever this is, but please Shorty, don't take away the pleasure of me being able to taste something good. Please." I begged and her face softened up.

I watched as she thought it over for a moment before letting out a slight sigh. "I am only going to give you a little bit." She said, giving in. I smiled for joy as she walked over and scooped all the food to one section on the divider and then filled the empty sections up with her food. My mouth began to salivate as the scent danced in my nostrils. "Don't take all day, I don't want her walking in on you eating it." She said while glancing at her watch. Little did she know I was about to inhale this food. "Slow down before you choke," she cautioned, but I was already done and licking the remains off the fork.

"Girl, I know you say you don't' have time for a man, but hell can I get that position." I joked as I laid back feeling satisfied.

"Now look at you all full and tired." She kidded while standing up. "I am going to wash the evidence out of your bowl. You get some rest." She said as she grabbed her things and my container. "Where do you want me to put this notebook?

"Just give it to me and I'll find somewhere to keep it." I said as I grabbed it and placed it on my lap. "You stacking these magazines gave me an idea, so tomorrow I am going to stack these pillows up and start writing." I continued and she smiled.

"Great and I'll bring the puzzles when I come Wednesday. Don't worry Spenc, we are going to get you up and moving in no time." She smiled again, finished straightening up the room and then left me to my own thoughts.

Chapter Two
July 25th, 2019

Alana

I sat behind the desk at the noisy police station. My morning was filled with filing papers, packing and sorting folders. This was just my second day on the job, and I was already up to my knees in work. Jody, the receptionist before me had been on sick leave for two weeks, but I did not imagine it would be all this work. Especially since nothing rarely happens in this little town.

"Hey Lanz," I heard a strong velvety voice say behind me.

I couldn't help but roll my eyes. "Here we go," I mumbled as Deputy Scott Lanson stepped into view. He was a full six feet, maybe two hundred pounds. You could tell he was mixed, because of his hazelish green eyes, lighter skin tone and curly hair. But his features were definitely of African descent. I could not lie he was a handsome devil, but he was cocky and that is one thing I could not stand in a man. "What do you need deputy," I said with a little attitude, hoping it would persuade him to walk away.

"Now why you always gotta treat me like that? "He questioned, while giving me his best smile.

"Like what?" I asked, innocently.

"Like you don't like me or something." He replied, sitting down on the corner of my desk.

I looked up at him. "It's not that I don't like you, it's just," I paused for a moment to choose my words correctly. "I am just really busy, and I don't have time right now."

"Well what about tonight?" He coaxed in the smoothest voice.

"What about it?" I asked and looked back down at the folder I was packing.

"Will you have time tonight?"

"I'm busy tonight," I replied dryly.

"With who? Spencer?" He mocked and I quickly looked up. I was so busy trying to ignore him that I didn't notice him pick up one of the word search books I had brought. "To Spencer, to help your mind stay focus." He read in a flirtatious tone.

"Give me that," I said while snatching it out of his hand. "Didn't your mother ever teach you to leave people stuff alone? I sneered, while stuffing the book in my bag.

"No, but she did teach me how to change my identity and not be found." He remarked.

I sat there uncertain of what to say next. "Boy, what? Stop talking crazy." I muttered and he smiled.

"I'm joking, but....um... for real." He muttered in a low tone before quickly changing the subject. "Who is Spencer and is he better looking than me?"

"Do I detect a hit of jealousy?" I mocked.

"Nope, just want to know who I gotta arrest so you can be free." He kidded and I laughed.

"Wow, abuse of power. I am going to write that up in the report." I joked and he laughed. "But if you must know, Spencer is this tall, dark and handsome man that lives up on Hill street." I said in the sexiest voice, hoping he would leave me alone.

"Oh, so you are dating a ghost." He clowned with a loud laugh.

"Wow, so you think the house is haunted as well. I never assumed you to be a scaredy cat."

"Ain't no one scared." He said while sitting up straight. I could tell I had offended his manhood. "What are you doing going up to the Hill house anyway?" His tone was full of envy.

I huffed and rolled my eyes. "I am taking care of Spencer; he was in a bad car accident and his wife hired me. He's having memory problems, so I get him these books to help him remember."

He raised his eyebrows and stared at me strangely. I couldn't help but feel a little bit attracted to him as I watched his facial movements. My mind started to wander as my eyes roamed his body. Maybe I could let him take me out. The thought crossed my mind, but I quickly shook it away.

"Alana, are you listening?" He asked, breaking me out of my thoughts.

"Huh, oh yeah. What did you say?"

"When was he in a car accident?"

"Sometime in May." I replied, not understanding why he was still looking lost.

"May?" He mumbled and I could feel myself getting irritated. He was acting as if I was speaking another language. I was about to say something to him, but my brother cut me off.

"Deputy, don't you have something better to do other than being in my little sisters face?" He said sternly and Scott quickly stood up.

"Oh, sorry Sheriff. Huh?" He called out while looking in the other direction. "You called me Larry?" He continued acting as if one of the other officers was talking to him. "Oh, yeah here I come." He said and quickly walked off.

"Really?" I said with a little laugh before looking at my brother, who just shook his head and walked away. I laughed again and continued to file the papers, but I couldn't help but think back to Scott and his confused face. Why was he so surprised to hear about a car accident? You would think he would have known about it. I am sure the police were called. Especially if he was rushed to the hospital. But then again, knowing Mr. Lanson, he was probably in some females face and missed the entire thing.

"I can't believe he thought I was dating Spencer." I muttered to myself as the possibility popped into my head. The two days I spent with him were the best moments of my week. He was funny, sweet, caring and for a person that couldn't remember much, he was a great conversationalist. Talking to him was like talking to an old best friend that I never knew I had, and I guess if the circumstances were different, maybe I would consider dating him. Hell, his wedding picture was fine as hell. I thought before snapping myself back into reality. "Get it together Lani, that is unacceptable." I checked myself really quick as the thought of Celeste popped into my head. She was too sweet of a person for me to be fawning over her husband.

"Let me get back to work," I mumbled to myself and continued to file papers. Filing away whatever thought I had of Spencer into the far back of my mind.

July 26th

Spencer

I sat back, watching her in the distance. Her thick hips swaying to the music and her chocolate skin gleaming under the dim light. I couldn't see her face, but I knew exactly who it was.

"Comes sit on my lap Shorty," My deep voice, sounded far away as she seductively walked closer to me. I rubbed my hand on my hard, thumping member. I couldn't wait to feel her warmth on mine.

"Good morning!" I heard Celeste manly voice call out, yanking me out of my peaceful slumber. I opened my eyes and then quickly closed them as she opened the blinds. I opened them again, slower, so they could adjust to the light. "Looks like someone is happy to see me this morning." She giggled while helping me sit up in the bed. It took me a minute to realize she was talking about my hard member, poking through the sheets.

"Oh, I'm sorry," I said as I quickly tried to adjust myself in the bed.

"You have nothing to be sorry about baby, it ain't like I haven't seen it before." She flirted, as she sat on the side of the bed and trailed her finger up my thigh. "Honestly, I am happy to see him growing, I was beginning to think you were not attracted to me anymore." She added with a pouted lip.

"Never that baby," I lied, while caressing her hand. Honestly, no matter how many times I see her, I could not really see myself being with her. I mean I get she was gorgeous back in the day, but I just can't believe I sat here all these years and watched her turn into what she was today. I mean, I don't know much about myself, but I knew that the person I could see myself with would be smart, funny and sexy. Kind of like Alana, she was everything I could ever want in a woman. Pretty, intelligent, caring and she was a go getter, out here going to school and working two jobs. That shit was a complete turn on.

"Oh my," Celeste said as my member began to grow harder against her hand. She quickly moved it and I watched her face turn a bright red. "Whew, Spencer." She panted in heat as she quickly got up to get my medicine together. She stepped out of view, and I quickly closed my eyes and tried to think of anything to put myself at ease.

I sat myself up in the bed and got ready for breakfast. "So baby, did you make the green veggie hash this morning like you did last Friday?" I asked, hoping to change the subject.

"You remember last Friday?" She asked in an uneasy tone.

"Well not all of it, just the beginning. Last week is starting to fill into my mind slowly. But some of it doesn't make sense?"

"What do you mean?" She asked in a light voice.

"Well, in my mind, I am remembering things as I had been here longer than a week or two. It starting to feel like months." I replied, not really knowing how to explain it.

"Oh wow, that is quite strange." She said in a neutral tone. "You are certainly, starting to remember a lot quicker. I hate that it's all disillusioned." She stated.

"Yeah, well, Alana has been helping me by doing some different memory exercises. So, by me remembering this much, they must be helping." I replied as I laid back a little and closed my eyes.

"Aw yes, Alana." She replied in an eerily calm voice. "I like her, she reminds me of a daughter I wish we had. She's so sweet and so helpful, I would hate to have to let her go." She continued.

"Why would you have to let her go," I said suddenly feeling the vibe in the room change. "Celeste?" I called out as I opened my eyes, surprised to see her standing right next to me.

"Yes, Spencer?" She said with a peculiar smile on her face. I suddenly felt nervous, as if I had seen this look before. But before I could sit up, an icy feeling flowed through my veins. My mind slowly faded to black.

Alana

Class ended five minutes late, so I had to move fast if I wanted to get up the hill on time. I made sure I had everything I needed before I left the house, so I didn't need to stop at home. Quickly running out of the building, I unlocked my doors, tossed my bag in the passenger seat, and zoomed out of the parking lot. I don't know why, but I was particularly excited to see Spencer today. I couldn't wait to hear about his crazy dreams and show him these new books.

I pulled up to the house a few minutes after two, parked, grabbed my things and shot up the stairs. To my surprise, Celeste was already standing in the doorway. Her eyes were red and sunken in.

"Oh my God Celeste." I panicked, throwing my bag further up my arm so I could comfort her. "What happened?"

"It's Spencer, he woke up this morning and cannot remember a thing." She cried out with a flushed face.

"Already?" I asked while helping her inside and closing the door. "I thought it took weeks before his mind erased?" I asked as I remembered a talk me and her had before.

I led her to the living room, and we sat on the couch. "Yes, I know." She rushed, "The doctor just left before you got here. He said that Spencer must have been overly stimulating his mind or something, But I don't know what he could have been doing, do you?" She asked with a raised brow.

I could feel my face drain as I thought about the memory exercises and the food I had been giving him. Could I have been the reason his memories faded so quickly. "Oh my God Celeste, I am so sorry. I was helping Spencer do mind games hoping it would assist him. If I am the reason he has forgotten then," I paused before standing up. "I understand if you would want me to go."

"No, Alana please do not be so dramatic." She said, grabbing my hand. "I would never ask you to leave. I love you being here. Just having you in our home, brings a little joy in our lives. You remind me of a daughter I once had." She confessed. "She would have been about eighteen this year."

I could feel my eyes widen. "You and Spencer had a child?" I whispered surprisingly, while sitting back down in the chair.

"Yes, Alyssa, was such a beautiful little thing, free and vibrant. Her little presence would light up the house as well." She said with a smile so wide that the corners of her eyes began to wrinkle. "But as always, tragedy struck in our family." She said and in that same instant her happy face filled with a devastating sadness.

"What happened?" I asked in a low voice.

"We looked for her for days and days, we thought she had run away. I would have rather she'd had run away." She said and her voice trailed off.

My heart grew heavy and my mind grew curious. I didn't want to ask her what happened, but I couldn't help myself. "Celeste, what happened to Alyssa?"

"We found her little five-year-old body, bent and broken in the well behind the shed." She said in a weird, cold hearted tone. "But here we are." She continued, standing up. "I am going to take you upstairs and reintroduce you to Spencer." She said in a cheery tone, as if we didn't just have the conversation about her daughter.

"Um, ok." I hesitated as I followed up behind her. I couldn't help but be taken back from the change in her manner, so much so that I barely said any words to Spencer when she introduced me again.

"Let's let him get his rest today," She said while closing the door. She turned around and we both walked down the stairs. "I will be home a little early today, I just have to take care of something simple. But I will still pay you for the entire day." She continued and before I knew it, she was out the door.

I stood in the middle of the room, slightly confused. I just couldn't get over the fact that she switched from devastated and sorrowful to upbeat and cheerful in the blink of an eye. This wasn't the first time I had noticed a quick change in her demeanor. Some days it really felt like I was talking to two different people. Something just didn't seem right, I thought as I looked around the big house. A chill ran through me as I thought about all the horror stories I've heard through the years. Hell, if I believed in that stuff, I would have thought she was possessed or something.

"Thank God I don't believe in those things." I said with a hesitant laugh, but I still felt weird. The last few days I was able to sit in the living room and study, but at this moment I didn't want to be alone. I glanced up the stairs and debated on if I should go talk to Spencer. Even though he didn't remember me, I am sure he was still the same Spencer I had grown to love.

After careful consideration, I decided to go against Celeste's orders. Taking another quick glance around the room, I swallowed the lump in my throat and headed up the stairs to visit Spencer. I knocked softly and waited for him to respond.

"Come in," I heard his groggy voice say behind the door.

"Hey Spenc," I cautioned while slipping into the room. Apart of me hoping that him hearing his nickname would spark some type of memories.

"Hey, Alana, right?" He said and I could feel my heart drop.

"Yeah, I'm Alana." I said as I pulled the recliner closer to the bed as I did the last two times I was here.

"Wow, you're a pro already huh?" He joked and I smiled.

"Yeah, I know about your restrictions," I said pointing to the bandages.

"Yeah, I can't stand it. But I'm hoping to start healing soon." He replied while laying back in the bed. I sat there for a while, oddly staring at him. "What's wrong, is there something on my face?" He kidded, and I felt a bit of happiness flow through me. At least he was his same funny self.

"You really don't remember anything?" I inquired, hoping this was just some kind of joke.

"Not really. Celeste tried to remind me of somethings this morning, but my mind is just blank. She said that you've been here taking care of me for a few days." He paused. "I don't know how I could forget someone as pretty as you though." He said with a smile and I laughed.

"Whatever Spenc," I replied, letting a little giggle escape my lips. He had never made a pass at me before and I don't know why it made me feel the way it did. I sat talking to him for a while, most of the conversation was the same as when I first met him, but it felt like we had not really missed a beat. "I bought you some food."

"I don't even think I can eat. I've been feeling sick all morning and I have the worst headache." He let out a disappointed sigh. "I am so tired of feeling like this. I just wish it were something I could do to help me with my memory." He said frustratingly.

"Well," I said but then quickly changed my mind. It was not my place to make that decision.

"Well what?" He quickly replied, but I shook my head to indicate that it was nothing. "No, you were about to say something." He paused, waiting for me to answer.

"It's nothing."

"Alana, sitting here with you talking the way we are, lets me know that we are a little closer than what I am remembering. If you know something that will help me, I need you to help me."

I stared into his pleading eyes and in that moment, I decided to once again go against Celeste's wishes. "Listen, I've been helping you with your memory the past couple of days by doing different memory exercises. But the doctor said that by doing so, it caused you to over stimulate your brain, which caused you to have a relapse. I don't want to be the cause of you losing any more of your memories." I explained and he looked at me strangely.

"The doctor said by doing mental exercises I was over working my brain, what sense does that even make?" He said, but I could tell he wasn't really asking me. "When did he say that?"

"I don't know, he wasn't here when I got here. I must have just missed him." I replied, not knowing what else to say. We both sat quiet for what seemed like an eternity. I could tell he was trying his hardest to remember something, anything. But he just continued to come up with blanks.

"So, what type of exercises where you doing with me?" He said breaking the silence.

"Well," I said while pulling out the puzzle books. "I gave you some puzzle books like these to complete, as well as a notebook so you could start writing your dreams and memories down.

"Well let me see the notebook," he said excitedly. I shook my head.

"I don't have it, you've hid them." I said and I could see the irritation spread across his face.

"Damn it!" He yelled, causing me to jump a little. "I am sorry, I am just mentally exhausted and physically weak. I don't understand why I am feeling like this when I was just only in a car accident a few weeks ago.

I was about to say something, but I quickly decided not to. I was already treading on thin ice, telling him the truth of how long it has really been was definitely not my place. "Here," I said while pulling out another notebook. "Take this one and maybe subconsciously you will hide it with the other." I said, standing up and catching a glimpse out of the window. "Shit," I muttered as I dodge back, pushing the recliner back as well. "Celeste is here, I have to go. I'll see you later." I tossed the notebook on the bed and quickly jetted out of the room, plopping down on the living room couch. I pulled out my book and pretended to read a page as the keys jingled in the door. I tried my hardest to look natural, but I felt like a fool.

"Hey, I am back." I heard Celeste say, followed by her heavy footsteps.

"Hey, you weren't playing when you said you will be here early." I replied once she peeked her head around the corner. I looked down at my watch and it was only four.

"Nope, I knew what I had to do wasn't going to take long." She paused. "But its Friday, you shouldn't be working late anyway. I know a beautiful thing like yourself has a boyfriend or something. Do you have any plans for the weekend?" She questioned as I started to pack my book bag.

"I don't really have any plans, but I did have someone ask me out." I paused and thought about Scott.

"Well, maybe you should except it and have some fun, kids now a days don't know how to have fun anymore." She replied coarsely.

"You know what, maybe I will." I said jumping up and tossing my bag on my back. "Maybe if I leave now, I can catch him." I continued as I headed towards the door.

"That's the spirit," she replied while following up behind me. I opened the door and stepped outside. It was warm and felt like a good day to get into something.

"Ok, Celeste I'll see you Monday."

"Ok see you then, have a safe drive," was the last thing I heard as I quickly ran down the stairs and headed to the station.

My stomach tied up in knots as I rounded the corner to the police station. I hadn't been on a date in months and now I was about to ask Scott if he wanted to go out. Getting myself together quickly. I stepped out of the car and smoothly walked inside.

"Where is he?" I mumbled to myself as I looked around the semi-empty station. His things were at his desk, but he was nowhere in sight. "Oh well," I muttered as I turned around to leave, but surprisingly bumped into something big and hard.

"Damn Lanz, I knew you wanted me, but I didn't know it was this bad." Scott joked, while holding me up. I wanted to say something, but the smell of his cologne was so enticing that it felt like I was in a Scott wonderland. "Hello, earth to Lanz." He continued and I quickly broke out of my trance.

"Oh, my bad. I guess your solid chest knocked some sense out of me."

He laughed and started walking towards his desk. "So, what are you doing here, I thought you had to work?" He asked, mockingly.

"I did, but I got off early and I came up here to see if," I paused hesitantly.

"If what?" He asked with a smirk.

"If, you know, you wanted to get some drinks or something tonight?" I replied nonchalantly, I didn't want him to sense how nervous I was.

"Oh, you want to go on a date with me." He cheesed, over doing his entire part in the conversation.

"If you are going to do all of that, then never mind." I said and got ready to make my exit.

"Wait, wait." He said while grabbing my hand and pulling me back. I could feel my body warm as his soft but masculine hand wrapped around mine. "Slow down girl," he said in a tone so smooth that my stomach started to flutter. "I'm just messing with you. I would love to go on a date with you. But," he paused and scrunched up his face. "I'm working the late shift tonight."

"Well how about tomorrow?"

"I can't, I am following up on a lead to a case I've been working on." He huffed and I could tell he wished he didn't have these prior arrangements.

"A lead to a case? Look at you, sounding like a real inner-city police officer. This little town may be too much for you." I joked, trying to hide my devastated feelings.

He laughed and then put his finger on his chin. "I have to drive to Phoenix. You should come with me." He suggested and I quickly shook my head no.

"Phoenix is a five-hour drive, no thank you." I said as pleasant as possible. I didn't want him to think I was coming off rude, but hell no I was not about to do a road trip with this man.

"Ok, well how about Sunday?"

"Sunday would be great." I replied with a smile and he smiled back.

"No," I heard a stern voice say and I looked over and saw my brother walking towards us. "No, she's finishing school without a baby." He said pointing at Scott. "Lani, go home." He said to me and before I could protest, he gave me that serious don't start with me look.

"Ight Dunc," I said and started to walk backwards, making sure to wink at Scott before I turned around.

"What did I tell you," I heard Duncan say to Scott in the distance before I walked out of the station.

I knew I was going to hear my brothers mouth later tonight, but I didn't care. I needed something different to get my mind off of everything. Seeing Spencer like that today really hurt me. I mean he did not remember anything about the last two days we spent with each other. It reminded me to much of my mother and I am really hoping he is not developing onset Alzheimer's like she did.

The thought of my mother didn't make me feel any better, I missed her so much. I hadn't gone to visit her at the nursing home in weeks. Every time the doctors thought she was getting better; her memory would get worst. The last time I was there she had completely forgotten who I was, and I just couldn't take seeing her like that anymore. My mother was my best friend and for her not to know me, hurt me to my soul. The thought of going to see her today crossed my mind, but I quickly sided against it. I couldn't handle seeing her, not right now.

July 28th

I walked into the dimly lit sports bar around eight. It was lightly crowded and didn't take me long to spot Scott sitting at the far end of the bar. I made my way through the tables and walked up to him. He stood up, gave me a small hug and then pulled out my chair. I couldn't help but stare at his strong, tatted up arms as they bulged through his short-sleeved shirt. I guess I never realized how built he was until now.

"You like what you see," he laughed, and I quickly took my gaze off his body. "You got some drool there." He joked, pointing to my lip.

"Shut up." I said and laughed embarrassingly at myself.

"You look nice," he flirted.

I could feel my face warming as a smile formed. "Thank you."

"You want a drink?" He asked and handed me the menu. "Bartender," he called out and a young lady quickly approached us. "Can I get a Hennessey and she'll have," he paused, waiting on my answer.

"A Hennessey margarita please." I replied and he looked at me and smiled.

"A woman after my own heart." He said shaking his head. "Angela," he said back to the bartender. "Let me get a jerk chicken plate with extra mac." He looked at me. "You want jerk chicken, ribs or catfish?" He asked and I picked the chicken as well. "Give her some extra mac too, because I'm not sharing mine when she dogs hers." He laughed and I shook my head.

"I don't even eat like that." I said when Angela walked away.

"Girl, you are Duncan's sister and I've seen the plates he brings to work. I know he ain't cooking like that, so I know you eat like that." He chuckled, with a smug smile.

"You think you cute don't you." I jabbed and he nodded his head.

"I don't think, I know." He replied and we both laughed again.

The bartender brought us our drinks and we sat there talking and chatting about our day. I couldn't help but stare at his lips as he spoke. My mind started to trail off and visions of us making out filled my thoughts. I tried to stay focus but seeing him out of uniform and in his natural setting was opening up feelings in me that I didn't know I had. My body parts were getting worked up with every smile he threw my way. I couldn't help but let out a sigh of relief when are food finally came out.

"Well damn," I said as I opened the Styrofoam container filled to the brim with Chicken, mac and cheese, red beans and rice and cabbage. My mouth began to water as the spicy aroma filled my nose. I was about to dig in, but Scott stopped me.

"Hold on Lanz, you are missing the best part." He said and grabbed the small plastic container that was filled with a semi thick brown sauce. "This is their homemade jerk sauce and it brings it all together." He added while pouring it over the chicken. "Now, that's a masterpiece." He said and we both dug in.

"Damn," I said as I took a few more bites before closing my container and putting it to the side. "That food is so good; I have to save it for later." I continued while wiping my fingers with what seemed like a thousand napkins.

"Yeah, I am just going to have to order me another one to go." He said and looked down at his plate, the only thing left was the bones of the chicken and the residue cheese from the mac. "Angela, let me get two shots of Hen." He called out and she came over and poured the shots. He grabbed his glass and pushed the other one closer to me. "To our first date," he continued while raising the small drink in the air.

To our first date," I repeated, and we clinked the little glasses together and tossed them back. "Smooth," I grunted, and he laughed.

"Oh really? Angela two more." He called out and we took them as well.

"If I didn't know any better, I would think you were trying to get me drunk." I giggled and then let out a little squeak. I was definitely feeling those two Margaritas I had before the food came.

"Naw, your brother would kill me if I did that." He said in a serious, but half-jokingly tone.

"My brother is not the boss of me, I am grown." I slurred a little and he laughed.

"I feel you ma." He paused and took a drink of his beer. It was no longer sweating so I knew it had to have been warm at this point.

"How was the trip?" I asked, as I sipped on the little bit of margarita I had left.

"It was cool, but it was a kind of a dead in."

"Why was it?" I asked genuinely interested.

"I didn't get the information I was looking for."

"Well, what were you looking for?" I asked hoping he would stop with the stalling answers and get to the nitty gritty. His forehead wrinkled as he debated on telling me, and then his lips formed into an excited smile.

"Ok look, a couple of days ago, we found this beat up moving truck. You could tell the driver must have lost control of it and went down the side of the road. Blood was in the car, but there was no driver in sight. At first, we thought it was some type of human smuggling situation gone wrong, but when we opened the back it was empty. I thought it was weird, so I searched the truck. It took a minute, but I found a business card to an apartment complex just a little bit outside of town." He explained with excitement.

I couldn't help but smile at his seriousness. I never knew he was into this detective type work. It was kind of sexy.

"What are you smiling about?" He asked in mid-sentence.

"Nothing, just enjoying the conversation. Continue, I'm listening."
I flirted and he smiled at me.

Ok, so I went and checked it out."

Checked what out?" I said, needing to be reminded of the last part of his story.

"The apartment complex." He repeated, and I nodded my head. "Ok, so I talked to the landlord and through simple conversation, he mentioned how a tenet had paid the rent up for six months, but never showed up." He went on, and I sat there with a confused look on my face, I couldn't help but wonder what all of this had to do with Phoenix. He must have noticed the look on my face because he smiled and said, "I know you are wondering what all of this has to do with Phoenix."

"And now I am wondering are you a mind reader." I joked and we both shared a laugh.

"The landlord also mentioned that the tenant was taking the truck back to Phoenix. I called around, looking for anyplace that was missing a truck and there was only one. So, I went to check it out, but it was a dead in." He finished, leaving me lost.

"Ok, you said all of that to say what?" I asked with a twisted look. He gave me all these pieces of information but clearly, I had missed something.

He looked around to make sure no one was listening and then leaned in closer to me. "I think our department has a missing person on our hands." He whispered, and I sat there in awe.

"Are you serious?" I asked while running the information back in my mind. "What makes you think that?"

"Random truck and a missing tenant that no one has heard from. What that sound like to you?"

"It sounds like you might be on to something Detective. Let's call Liv and Fin in on the case." I joked, with a sly smile.

"Yeah... yeah... yeah. Very funny. But with all this stuff on the news about that lady killing all those people.

"The Tender Killer," I noted.

"Yeah, her. I wouldn't be surprise if the person missing was one of her victims." He concluded while shaking his head.

An eerie chill ran through my body as I sat there processing the facts. I had been following the news and The Tender Killer case was getting weirder by the day.

"My bad." Scott said, breaking the silence between us.

"For what?" I asked, while holding up my hand and letting the waiter know I needed another drink.

"For making the mood so heavy, we were having a good time and I had to bring up some crazy mess." His tone was low and gloomy.

"Boy, you did not mess up the mood, hell if anything you added a little spunk." I said hoping to make him feel a little better.

"Ok good. But look, you can't tell anyone about my findings. Your brother told me not to waste my time with it and I don't want him to know about it until I know for sure what's happening.

"Ok, I will keep it to myself." I replied and we sat quietly for a few seconds.

"Can I ask you a question?" He asked, breaking the silence.

"Yeah?" I replied as the bartender handed me my drink.

"What made you wanna go out with me?" He asked, and I was so caught off guard by the question that I choked a little on the drink

"Oh, um." I paused and tried to find the right words to say. I figured since he opened up to me about his case, I could open up to him as well. "Well, you know I am working for this client." I started and he nodded his head. "Well her husband was in a car accident and he lost his memories. I met him Monday and by Friday he had completely forgotten me. Seeing Spencer like that, not being able to remember anything, not even new memories." I stopped and shook my head. "It made me realized how much I've been taken my life for granted."

"Damn," he murmured in disbelief. "So, he starts new memories and then forgets them as well. That is some lifetime movie network mess right there.

"I know right. And that ain't the only thing." I hushed and he leaned in closer. "His wife, Celeste, is the nicest… weirdest person I have ever met."

"What makes her weird?"

"She does this thing where she like changes characters. Sometimes she is this hoarse talking, clumsy walking woman with a hump." I tried to explain the best way I could.

"Sounds like the hunchback of Notre Dame." He joked and I shook my head trying to hold in the laugh that was starting to erupt. He was right, she did resemble the hunchback.

"I know right. But then other times she's this poise standing, pleasant talking Carol from the Brady Bunch. It's so weird how she turns it on and off. It gives me the willie nillies." I shook my head, before eating the cherry that was left at the bottom of the drink.

"Yeah, that does sound weird." He replied with a lifted eyebrow.

"I know right," I continued to tell him about my clients. At this point I knew I was drunk because I was spilling way too much information. I went from talking about Celeste and Spencer, to talking about my mom and even at some point I think I started crying. When I finally finished, Scott was staring at me like a crazy person. "Oh no, I over did it didn't I?" I slurred and he just shook his head.

"Naw, you good Lanz, come on let me help you get home." He said, while standing up and helping me off the stool. He wrapped my arm around his neck, and we stumbled out of the bar.

"Why officer, what did I do." My tone was of a sloppy drunk college chick. "Are you going to frisk me?" I flirted while rubbing my hands on his chest.

After gently fighting off my roaming hands, he finally got me to the car. He laughed as he opened the door and lightly pushed me inside. "Your brother is going to kill me," was the only thing I heard before he closed the door.

Scott Lanson

After safely getting Lanz home and thanking God that her brother
was not there. I pulled up to my little studio apartment and went
inside. Turning on the light, I walked into the kitchen and put my
extra plate into the fridge. I continued into the bathroom, turned on
the shower and got undress. I can't believe Lanz got that drunk, I
thought as I stepped under the warm water.

Thoughts of the night circled in my mind as the water beat down
on my head. I couldn't get over the things she was saying about her
clients. You have a woman that is clearly bipolar and then you
have a man that memory restarts every few days. Stories like that
only happen on tv, so I knew something wasn't right.

Suddenly a thought ran across my mind. I do not remember getting
any calls about a car accident. The only accident that we know
about is the moving truck on the side of the road.

"Wait a minute." I said aloud as my thoughts ran wild. Maybe it
was time for me to visit the house on the hill and do a little
investigating of my own. I made a mental note, to write down the
information she told me, finished my shower, and got straight in
the bed. It had been a long weekend and I needed my rest for
whatever I was about to encounter tomorrow.

I woke up the next day around ten, called into work for a sick day and then made me a nice breakfast. "Today might be a test of strength." I said as I shoved a forkful of eggs in my mouth. The loud jingle from my phone went off, indicating that I had a message. It was from Lanz, she was apologizing about last night. I assured her it was ok, and I let her know I couldn't wait for date number two. After I finished eating and cleaning up the house. I got dressed and headed on my mission.

I decided to take the back way up the hill so no one would see me coming. Once I got a little past the mid-way point. I pulled to the side and turned off the engine. I glanced at the clock; it was thirty minutes past one. I remember Lanz said she had to be at work at two, so I wanted to be gone before she got here.

I looked at my phone, my battery was draining. I always forgot to shut down my apps. "I'm not going to be here that long anyway." I muttered before placing the phone into my back pocket. I grabbed the flashlight, got out and stalked up the rest of the hill. It took me about ten minutes to reach the top. I tried to avoid the windows as I cased the parameter of the house. I didn't know what I was looking for, but I knew it was something out here to find.

As I rounded the side of the house, I noticed a small wooden shed, a little bit of ways down the hill. I checked around to make sure no one was watching before I ran towards the doors and swiftly slipped inside. The shed was dark, and the smell of dampness filled the air. I turned on my flashlight and went on the search.

The pounding of my heart, echoed through my ears as I looked around the weirdly decorated shed. It didn't look like a shed at all, but more like a small room. There was a table filled with medical instruments and a stretcher sitting oddly in the middle of the room.

"Could this be some sort of self-made hospital torture chamber?" I asked myself as I walked further inside. In the corner was a big metal table, it was bolted to the floor and covered in jars. I hesitantly reached out to grab one of them, but I could feel the fear rising in my body. A part of me just knew I was about to find some damn eyeballs floating in gel or something. "Here goes nothing," I mumbled as I grabbed the jar and opened it up.

To my surprise, it wasn't eyeballs, but a jar full of urine. I could feel myself getting nauseated as I quickly placed it on the shelf. I was about to grab another jar, but a creaking sound from behind startled me.

"You shouldn't be in here," I heard a pleasant voice say and I quickly turned around. I was surprised when I saw this manly woman standing there, from the sound of the voice I really expected someone smaller. She stood oddly in the doorway with her hands behind her back.

"Oh, sorry ma'am. I am deputy Lanson and I am investigating a missing person's report. I only came in here because I thought I heard something strange. I was actually on my way to knock on your door." I lied, hoping she would just escort me to the house. She didn't say anything, she just stared at me with a twisted smile over her face.

I could feel the hairs on the back of my neck stand up as her eyes pierced my soul. "Ma'am?" I called out as I walked closer to her. "Don't worry about it, I'll just come back another time." I continued, making the effort to get past her.

"There won't be another time." She said and revealed a shiny kitchen knife from behind her back. I was about to say something, but she launched at me, swinging the blade like a mad woman.

"Hey lady," I yelled while quickly moving and dodging out of her way. "Damn," I screamed out when the blade swiped against my arm. It was at that moment, my adrenaline really kicked in and I took off towards her, knocking her down as I pushed past the door.

I looked back and saw her behind me, chasing me up the hill with a shovel. I looked forward and from a distance I could see a car coming up the hill. My heart raced when I noticed it was Lanz. At the angle I was running I could see her, but I knew she couldn't see me. I put all my might into picking up my speed.

"Alana," I yelled out, hoping she would hear me. I looked back and I didn't see the lady behind me, but I didn't want to take any chances. "Alana," I called out again, but this time waving my hands. She still didn't see me. I was getting ready to call her again when bam, I was out like a light.

I opened my eyes and looked around. "What the hell," I mumbled to myself. I was still in a daze from being hit, but I could tell I was back in the shed, but this time I was handcuffed to the metal table. "Damn it!" I yelled, while yanking at the cuffs. Fear rose inside of me as I frantically tried to see through the darkness. "What can I do?" I grunted as I tried to look around for something, anything to help me get lose. I slid my hand on the floor, but I didn't feel anything that could save me. Sweat dripped down my forehead as I yelled and screamed for help. I continued until my throat was sore, but I knew no one was around to hear me. I continued to yank, pull and push at the handcuffs until my hands were raw and bloody, but no matter what I did. I couldn't get lose.

After struggling with the handcuffs and trying my hardest to get my phone out my back pocket, I was physically and mentally beat. I finally stopped fighting, took a deep breath and tried to calm my nerves.

"Are you done?" I heard the pleasant voice followed by the creaking of the door.

"Let me go, I am an officer and you will go to jail for detaining me." I yelled and she just stared at me with her same twisted smile. "Why are you doing this?" I asked as she walked over to me with her hands behind her back. "Get away from me." I continued to yell as she got closer and closer.

I watched in horror as she pulled a long syringe from behind her back. "Now this is just some numbing medication. You will be able to hear and see but you won't be able to move." She said in a song like voice before jabbing the needle into my arm. It hit me almost instantly as I felt my body go limp.

She walked over to me and kicked my leg, I guess to see if the medication worked. I watched as she laid a large blanket on the floor and then walked over to uncuff my hands. I felt totally helpless. How did I get myself in this situation, why was I so hell bent on coming up here and trying to solve a mystery? I had heard all the ghost stories about hill house and now I am about to become one of them.

I could feel the tears forming in my eyes as the thoughts raced through my head. I could not believe this was happening and I just wanted to wake up from this nightmare. "You don't have to do this, if you let me go, I promise I won't come back, and I won't tell anyone about it." At this point I was frantic and was willing to say anything to her. I kept trying to move my body parts as I talked, but nothing worked.

I continued to beg and plead for my life as she uncuffed me from the table and used her strength to cuff my hands behind my back. I grunted as she pushed me down to the floor, rolling me into the blanket as if I were a dead dog. I knew in that moment, I was going to die, and this lady was going to be the one to do it.

I was so busy in my thoughts that I didn't realize the feeling was starting to come back in my hand. I looked around and the lady was standing with her back to me. I wiggled my fingers until they were in my pocket. I could feel my phone, but I couldn't slide it out. I stopped moving when she turned around and headed back over to me.

"What are you doing?" I asked as she tossed a shovel in the blanket with me and walked towards my legs. I tried to move but I couldn't. She grabbed the ends of the blanket and slowly dragged me out of the shed. "Where are you taking me?" I yelled, but she ignored. "Think Scott, think." I whispered to myself, hoping something, anything would just pop in my head.

My hand was still in my pocket and I could feel the soft rubber buttons on the side. A thought popped into my head causing me to remember something my mother taught me. If you press the power button three times in a row on an android phone, it sends out an SOS to my emergency contact. I couldn't even remember if I had set it up or not and I wasn't sure if my phone was dead, but I was going to try anyway. I quickly pressed the buttons three times.

"What the hell are you doing?" The crazy lady roared, she must have saw my hand moving.

"Help me, help me somebody I am at the-" before I could finish my statement, I felt the weight of her heavy foot kick me in the side. I tried to catch the breath she had knocked out of me, but all I could do was gasp. She reached down to grab the phone out of my pocket. But with the help of God himself, I pulled my leg back and kicked her right in the chest.

The sound of her falling to the ground was all the motivation I needed as I scuffled to my feet. Dragging my half-numbed body, I ran up the incline as fast as I could. The side of the house came into view and from the distance, it looked like someone was standing in the window.

"Help!" I yelled but I knew I had to be closer. I went to scream one more time, but I felt something hard and metal hit me in the back of the head. The warm feeling of blood trickled down my face as I fell to my knees. I saw a pair of legs in front of me. I looked up, but my vision was blurry. The lady rolled me with her foot and I could feel myself tumbling back down the hill.

Chapter Three

Alana

I pulled up to the house, hopped out and ran up the long stairway. The teacher let us out of class early and I was actually able to get here on time. I rang the bell and waited for a few seconds for Celeste. It surprised me that she wasn't already at the door, waiting. Glancing at my watch, I tapped my foot eagerly on the wooden porch. I couldn't wait to sit down with Spencer and have are weekly chats. I wondered if I should tell him about Scott.

"No that would be kind of awkward." I mumbled and then looked at the time again. About a minute had rolled past and there was still no answer.

I rang the bell again.

This was not like Celeste at all, it had never taken her this long to answer the door. I began to get nervous. I walked over to the end of the porch and peeked around the side of the house, but I didn't see anything. When I turned back around, I was startled to see Celeste standing there with a shovel in her hand. She was sweaty and out of breath.

"Oh my God! Girl you just scared the hell out of me." I yelled, clutching my chest.

She looked at me strangely.

"Oh, we don't use that kind of language around here young lady."
She said in her pleasant voice. I quickly apologized and followed
her back to the door.

"Are you ok, today?"

"Oh yes, I was just in the backyard doing some gardening." She
replied as she set the shovel by the door and went inside.

"Oh, I didn't know it was a garden back there. I would love to see
it sometime." I said as I followed behind her.

"Oh," she paused as if she was thinking of something to say.
"Speaking of gardening, have you been giving Spencer any outside
food? He has been complaining of stomach pain." She asked,
completely changing the subject.

"No, ma'am I haven't given him anything." I lied, even though I
had pot roast and mashed potatoes in my bag with his name on it.

"Hmm…" she said and then walked into the kitchen. I sat my bags
down and pulled out my workbook. "Alana, I am going to be out in
the shed for a few, and then I will be heading into town. Can you
be a dear and just keep Spencer company. I will let you know
when I leave." She said and then I heard the back door open and
close.

I waited for a few minutes to see if she was going to come back or
not. When she didn't, I hesitantly walked up the stairs. A strange

feeling ran through my body as I thought about Celeste's request. Any other day she would tell me to let Spencer rest, today just seemed unusual. I stopped as an eerie chill creeped up my neck. I quickly looked behind me, but no one was there.

I continued up the stairs. "Spencer you woke?" I asked while knocking on the door.

"Yeah, come in." He replied and I opened the door. I was surprised to see his food still in front of him. Usually by this time everything would be cleaned up.

"Were you eating this by yourself?" I asked, while walking over to him and grabbing the tray.

"No, Celeste had set it up and then she ran out of here really fast and never came back. But I didn't want it anyway." He shrugged his shoulders.

"That's odd, she just told me she was out back doing some gardening."

"Gardening?" He said with a contorted face, "Celeste can barely cook, so I know she ain't gardening." He joked and I let out a hesitant laugh. "Alana, lighten up. Sometimes Celeste just does weird things."

"Like what?" I asked while sitting down in the recliner.

"Like talking to herself, pacing the house in the middle of the night and things like that. The doctor said it was because of her diagnosis."

"What diagnosis?"

"She has a bi-polar disorder." He said in a tone as if I should have known.

"Oh, I didn't know that, but I guess that does make sense." I replied as I got more comfortable in the chair. I pulled out my phone and pulled up the message thread between me and Scott. I had sent him an apology message and he replied, but he's been ghosting me since.

"Why the long face?" Spencer asked, breaking me out of my thoughts.

"It's nothing." I replied with a heavy sigh.

"What's his name?" He said in a knowingly tone and all I could do was smile. Spencer was starting to be like another brother to me.

"Scott." I said with a shy smile.

"The deputy, all nah Shorty, tell me it isn't so."

"What did you call me?" I exulted, while standing to my feet.

"I'm sorry, did I offend you?" He quickly apologized and I shook my head.

"I think you are starting to remember." I squealed and I could see a smile form across his dry lips. "You were calling me Shorty before," I paused. "Before you forgot again." I said hesitantly.

"Wait, I thought this was a celebration." He replied as he noticed the big change in my mood.

"No, Celeste said every time you start to really remember, you wake up the next day with everything gone again."

"Every time? How many times have I forgot?" He asked with a screwed-up face.

"I don't know how many times other than just recently. You would really have to ask Celeste." I replied, not really wanting to be the bearer of bad news.

"You know what, how about we just keep it our little secret for now. I just want to see something." He said in an uneasy tone and I nodded my head. I watched as he pulled out the second notebook, I had given him. He had hidden it inside of his pillowcase, which I thought was clever. He flipped to a new page and started recording.

"Wow, you've really been writing." I noted, while looking at all the pages that were now on the left side of the book.

"I write everything down, my dreams, my conversations and any little things that I notice." He said without looking up at me,

There was an awkward silence in the room, and I felt weird just staring at him writing. "You know what, I am going to take these dishes to the kitchen." I said, grabbing the bowl and quickly heading out the room. I took a deep breath as I walked into the kitchen. I don't know what it is about today, but I swear everything just seemed off.

I emptied the food into the garbage and sat the dishes in the sink. I stared out the window that was right above it, daydreaming. Memories of last night fluttered through my mind as I turned and aimlessly walked over to the refrigerator. My skin warmed as I thought about Scott's soft touches.

"Whew, Child." I gasped while grabbing the lemonade. I definitely needed something cold to cool me down, and this drink would have to do. "Damn, Celeste always makes the best lemonade." I said to myself as the sweet scent filled my nose. I poured a glass, put the jug back into the refrigerator and leaned with my back up against the sink. Pulling out my phone, I scrolled through social media as I sipped on the refreshing treat.

I thought I heard something in the distance, so I looked up from the phone and leaned forward a little to see if someone was in the front. "Celeste, is that you?" I called out, but I didn't get a response. "Hmph," I sighed and finished up my drink. When I turned around, I saw Celeste walking down the hill with a shovel in her hand. Hell, maybe it really is a garden down there somewhere. I finished up in the kitchen and then headed back up the stairs to keep Spencer company.

*****

I walked into the station, expecting to see Scott's smiling face. But not only was he not there, it looked as if his desk hadn't been touched in days. I got a weird feeling as I walked over to the receptionist desk. I sat down in the chair and switched the phone board over from nights to days. Since I was still the only receptionist, the night option lets the calls go to any phone in the station.

The phones started ringing almost instantly. I glanced over at Scott's desk one more time before picking up the call, "Hello,"

"Oh my God, finally! I've been calling all morning." I heard an agitated voice say on the other in.

"Sorry ma'am, the station has been busy this morning. Is there anything I can help you with?"

"Yes, earlier today I found a strange message on my phone. It was sent to me by my son and it sounded like he was in trouble."

"What type of trouble?" I asked, while grabbing a piece of paper and pen to write down the information.

"I don't know, it was muffled, kind of sounded like a butt dial. But I could hear him screaming. Or I think he was screaming." She hesitated.

"So, you are not sure what you heard?" I asked in a skeptical tone.

"I know what I heard!" She exploded, causing me to jump and pull the phone back from my ear.

"Listen ma'am, yelling is not going to help the situation. I just want to get all the facts straight. Now you said it sounded like a butt dial and that you were not sure if you heard him screaming. Do you think he might have just been out having a good time?" I asked, trying my hardest not to sound rude.

"Listen you little twat, please do not try to pacify me and make it seem like I am crazy. Obviously, you are to incompetent to understand what I am saying to you. But don't worry, I got it handled." She yelled and followed it up with the dial tone. All I could do was stare at the phone in disbelief before putting it back on the receiver.

The sound of the station's door opening, and closing made my heart skip. I smiled and waited to see Scott's handsome face, but my mood changed when I realized it was just my brother.

"Were you expecting someone else?" He asked with a sly smile.

"Not at all." I said, and he gave me the side eye, but I ignored it. "Hey, where is the deputy?" I asked in the most nonchalant voice I could muster up.

"I don't know, I was going to ask you the same thing." He said with an all knowing look on his face.

"Why are you looking at me like that?" I asked, still trying to play the nut role.

He scrunched his face up, "Come on Lani, this is a small town and people talk. You really think I wasn't going to hear about your drunken night with my deputy." He paused and I just shook my head in shame. "Now I heard he was a complete gentleman and he got you home safe, so I am not upset about that. I even understand why he called off yesterday, hell if I was him and I bought my boss' sister home drunk I would've called off too. But I don't understand why he isn't here today; he didn't even call the station."

"I haven't heard from him since yesterday morning," I replied. "Do you think he's ok?"

"I'm sure he is fine; I'll drop by his house while I'm out on patrol." He paused, noticing the fearful look on my face. "Sis, calm down. I am sure he is ok." He assured, but I couldn't shake the feeling that something was wrong. I thought about the last thing me and Scott talked about. What if he was on to something and his digging landed him in trouble. I wanted to tell my brother about Scott's outside investigations, but I also wanted to wait until I at least knew if Scott was home playing hooky. I decided that if Scott wasn't found by tomorrow, I was going to tell my brother everything.

*****

My alarm went off at its normal time, but instead of jumping right up, I laid there restless. I had tossed and turned all night; I couldn't help but think something bad had happened to Scott. I don't know where the feeling was coming from, but all I could think about was him being abducted by the Tender Killer for snooping in matters that didn't involve him.

I grudgingly pulled myself out of the bed and walked into the bathroom. I couldn't help but notice my bloodshot red eyes as I stared in the mirror. When Duncan came in at midnight and told me he still hadn't heard from Spencer, I couldn't stop my mind from thinking the worst. It took me all night, but I decided that I was going to let Duncan know everything Scott had told me.

I finished up in the bathroom and then went looking for Dunc. I searched the whole house, but it was empty. "He must have gone into work early." I said to myself before quickly getting ready and heading out the door.

Pulling up to the station about thirty minutes later, I jumped out of the car and rushed inside. "Oh, sorry." I quickly apologized to a man that I bumped into. I looked at him and he was standing in the doorway with a lost expression plastered on his face.

"Hey, I have a question," he said but I ignored him. I was on a mission and my main focus was to find my brother. I caught a glimpse of him sitting on the corner of his desk looking at a file.

"Duncan," I huffed out of breath.

"Hey sis, what's going on?" He asked, standing up and grabbing me by my shoulders. I could tell he was worried; I could see it in his eyes. I was getting ready to tell him everything, but I was cut off.

"Hey, is the sheriff here, I need some help." I heard a man's voice and I turned around. It was the guy I had bumped into. He was short, skinny and had like a Cherokee vibe going on with his reddish-brown skin tone, curly fro and beard. I had lived in this town a long time and I had never seen this person before.

"Hold on Lani," Dunc said, holding up one finger. "Hey, I'm Sheriff Duncan Johnson, what can I do for you?" He asked with his hand extended.

"Hey, my name is Kaden Bishop I am here to file a missing person's report." He said while shaking my brother's hand. I stood in shock as they both walked over to the desk.

"Ok. Lani, grab me a missing person file with all the paperwork inside." Dunc said and I quickly grabbed the folder from the file cabinet and handed it to him.

"Ok, who do you think is missing?" He asked while opening the folder and clicking the pen. I couldn't stop myself from shaking as I thought about Scott. He knew it was a missing person in this town and now someone has come looking.

"My brother Daniel Thompson, he sent a distress call to our mom and it sounded as if he was screaming. She's very worried and we just want to find out what's going on. She's been calling his phone, but it has been going straight to voicemail." He explained and I thought back to the call that had come in yesterday.

"What about the distress call made you think he was here in this town?" Duncan asked, while writing down the notes.

"Well, it sent the location of this town to her phone, as well as pictures." Kaden replied.

"What were on the pictures?" Dunc asked, looking up from the paperwork.

"Nothing, they were just dark. My mom thinks the phone was in his pocket." Kaden responded and then glanced over at me and then back at Dunc.

"I know almost everyone in this town, but I have never heard the name Daniel Thompson. What about you Lani?" Dunc asked while looking at me, I shook my head no.

"I have a picture of him," Kaden replied and pulled his bookbag off his back. Both me and my brother waited patiently as he pulled out a folder and flipped through it. I watched as he pulled the picture out and handed it to Duncan. The distraught expression on his face made me weary, so I moved closer so I could see the picture as well.

"Oh my God." I cried out in shock. "That's Scott!" I shrieked and I could feel my body growing cold.

"Scott?" Kaden asked with a confused brow.

"Yeah, Scott Lanson, he's the deputy." Duncan replied.

"And he's missing." I chimed in.

"We don't know that." Duncan said, while giving me the side eye.

"Well," I said, letting him know with my eyes that I knew something more.

"Well what, what's going on?" He asked in a slight panic.

"I think he might have been kidnapped by the Tender Killer." I replied and they both looked at me crazy.

"No, that can't be. The Tender Killer is locked up awaiting trial." Duncan replied with a 'what are you talking about' look on his face.

"She's not in jail," Kaden chimed in. "She was sent to a mental institution about a month or two ago."

"We haven't heard anything like that?" Duncan argued.

"Listen, I know the lawyer that was working on the case. Believe me she pled insanity and that's where they sentenced her." He explained.

"Ok. See Lani, so it can't be that." Duncan said bringing his attention to me.

"Well maybe it was someone associated with her." I stammered; I was so nervous that I couldn't get my words out.

"What reason would she have to come after Daniel?" Kaden jumped in.

"He was investigating a moving truck that was left on the side of the road." I started to say, but Duncan cut me off.

"No, I told him that was nothing to worry about."

"I know what you told him, but it did worry him, and he went on the search and found out that there was a person missing." I replied and then went into the details that Scott had told me a few days ago. "Somebody must have found out Scott was snooping around and got him." I finished and they both looked at me with wide eyes.

"Awe man, Scott. Why didn't you just tell me what you found," Duncan said while shaking his head. "Ok, Kaden, we are going to find your brother. We can head over to his house and see if we can find what he was working on and maybe it can lead us somewhere."

"That's cool with me." Kaden said and they both got ready to head towards the door.

"Wait for me." I said and followed up quickly behind them.

Duncan turned to me and a look of disapproval spread across his face, "No, hell no. You stay your little ass here. Matter of fact, take your ass to work." Duncan never cursed at me, so to hear him speak that way let me know that he was serious. "I'm sorry, this is just a severe police matter and I don't want you to get hurt."

"But he ain't a police officer." I argued, pointing at Kaden. I wasn't trying to be difficult, but I really wanted to know what was going on with Scott...or...um...Daniel.

"Alana," he said in a frustrated tone. "Go to work."

I huffed as he turned around and walked out of the station with Kaden.

"Go to work," I mocked while folding my arms. I didn't even know why I was upset; Duncan was right. I would just be in the way. I decided it was best for me to just stay here and keep an eye on the station until it was time for me to go see Spencer.

I drove up the hill and parked a little bit down the road. It was a little before two and I wanted to get myself together before I made it to the house. The side of the house was visible from where I was sitting, but I knew my car couldn't be seen from the angle of the street. Taking a deep breath, I pulled down the visor and flipped open the mirror. I stared at my tear stained face; I just couldn't get over the fact Scott was missing. I was just with him and we had such a good time.

I admit, when I first met him, I thought he was some type of smooth-talking ladies' man. But being with him Sunday night showed me a completely different side, and now he's missing.

I took another deep breath and grabbed some napkins out of the glove department to clean my face. Once I looked a little more presentable, I closed the visor. I could feel my expression hardening as I caught a glance of Celeste coming out of the basement cellar. She was wearing a hairnet and one of those aprons you would see at a slaughterhouse. She also had on a face mask and some gloves.

"What the hell is she doing?" I asked myself as I watched her carry a big bucket to the shed.

I sat there with a million and one things running through my mind as I waited for her to come out. Like what was she doing in the cellar and why was she dressed like she just gutted a pig. I remember her saying that the basement had mold, so maybe she was cleaning.

"Yeah, that's it, she's probably just cleaning." I tried way too hard to convince myself. I sat up to get a better view and then waited for Celeste to appear.

I glanced down at the clock. It had been about ten minutes and Celeste still hadn't come out. In that moment, I decided it was best to mind my business and go to work. Putting my foot on the break, I reached down to put the car in drive. Celeste popping out of the shed caught my attention. She was no longer dressed like a farmer but was now wearing a nice sundress and a bouncy wig. It was as if she went in one person and came out another. I don't know why, but it seemed so odd. So many questions ran through my mind, but I decided to shake them off. I waited a few seconds before pulling off and continued up the hill.

Celeste was already at the screen door waiting for me. I was surprised to see that she was wearing a full face of makeup, but I could tell by the look on her face that something was wrong.

"What's going on Celeste," I asked, while walking into the house. We went into the living room and sat on the couch as we always do.

"I don't know, I just feel like I slept too long. It's already two o clock." Her coarse tone was uneasy as she looked cluelessly around the house.

"What do you mean?" I asked just as clueless as her.

"I mean, I remember helping Spencer this morning. His memory reset and he woke up so agitated, that I had to give him a sedative. I was so worn out from helping him that I went into my room and laid down. And now I am down here with you." She said as she looked awkwardly around the living room. "I feel like my whole day has just disappeared somehow," she said as she covered her face with her shaky hands and started to sob.

I wanted to tell her that she was just outside looking like she kills cattle, but I decided against it. I thought back to what Spencer had told me and I realized she was probably having an episode. "It's ok Celeste," I said as I got up to comfort her.

"This has been happening a lot lately. I've been nauseated, I've been having these headaches and I've been missing chunks of time. I think I am going crazy." She said while looking up at me, black tears running from her mascara filled eyes. "It's ok, maybe it's just your condition." I said and she looked at me strangely.

"Condition?" She croaked.

"Yes, Spencer told me about your diagnosis, this could be a symptom of it." I paused when I saw the look on her face. "He didn't mean to tell me it just slipped out." I said trying to cover my tracks. Obviously, she didn't want anyone to know.

"She sat there for a minute just staring at me. I was starting to feel an awkward vibe and I really wish I could go back in time and not reveal her secret. "Celeste, I am going to grab you something to wipe your face and maybe something to drink." I said before hurrying to the kitchen.

I opened the refrigerator and was surprised when I didn't see the jug of lemonade. I knew it had to have been an off day, it had never been a time where I came, and she didn't have refreshments. I opened the cabinet and grabbed the jug, the lemonade powder and some glasses. I pulled open the drawer to grab a spoon but was shocked to see a cracked cell phone sitting inside.

I pulled it out and observed it. It was a regular android phone, but it had some dark dried up residue on it. I pressed the button to turn it on and it began to start up.

"You know what I am feeling a lot better." I heard Celeste pleasant voice behind me, causing me to jump a little. She glanced down at my hand and noticed the phone. "Oh, I see you found Spencer's phone, it got broken during the crash." She continued as she grabbed it out of my hand. She quickly put it in her pocket before I could see the lock screen. It seemed to me like she was lying, but I didn't want to make it obvious that I felt some type of way.

"Oh wow, that sucks. Well you know it's a little place in town where you can take it to get fixed." I said as I grabbed the jug and brought it over to the sink. I could feel her hovering behind me as I filled the jug with water. Nervousness slowly crept through me, causing the hairs on my arm to stand. I tried to keep my composure. "What are your plans today?" I asked, trying to get the tension out of the room.

"Well," she started to say before grabbing the jug from me. I watched as she continued to make the lemonade herself. "Today, I am just going to go visit my friend. I try to go and check on her at least two times a week. Her family forgot about her and she just sits in her room all day lonely and bored. So, I go see her to make sure she knows that I will never forget about her." She said while staring at me, her voice had somewhat of a dark undertone. It made me feel a little uncomfortable.

"Oh, well that's very nice of you," I replied with a forced smile. She smiled back but didn't reply. The room was quiet. The only other sound was the spoon hitting the jug as she stirred. She never took her eyes off of me, the weird smile plastered on her face made me uneasy.

The entire scene felt strange to me, so I excused myself and went back into the front. I pretended to look for something in my bag, but still kept watch of the door. I could still see her out of the corner of my eye, and she was still staring at me, smiling. At this point I was creeped out. I continued to look in my bag and prayed that she was getting ready to leave soon.

"All done," I heard her say and it startled me. I didn't even hear her come into the living room. "Alana, you are so jumpy today, is everything alright?" She asked while handing me a cup of juice.

"Yes, everything is fine," I replied, while grabbing the cup. She stood there with her back straight and her hands folded in front of her. She stared me down as if she were waiting for me to take a sip. I hesitantly put the cup to my lips, but it felt like I was about to drink to my death. I took a sip and then smiled. "Mmmhmmm" I replied, and she smiled back.

"Awesome," she said before grabbing her umbrella. "I heard it's supposed to rain today, so I won't be gone long." She said before heading out of the door.

Once I heard the door close, I spit the juice back in the cup. "I don't know what the hell that was about, but she ain't about to have me drinking the Kool-aid." I said before standing up and heading upstairs. I knocked on Spencer's door, but when I didn't get an answer I just peeked into the room. Spencer was laying flat on his back, sleeping, I had never seen him sleep in this late, but then I remembered she said she gave him a sedative.

"Where the hell did she get a damn sedative anyway?" I asked myself as I closed the door. The house was an unusual quiet, I guess I wasn't used to just being here with nothing to do. I would always spend my time talking to Spencer. I pulled out my phone and walked back to the front room. Plopping on the couch, I pulled up social media and started to scroll aimlessly.

I could feel my stomach start to growl around three, so I decided to heat my lunch up. I grabbed it out of my bag, walked in the kitchen and put it in the microwave. I leaned back on the counter and waited for the timer to go off. I started to think back to Celeste and how weird she was acting and then my eyes fell on the basement door. What could be down there? I thought as I walked over to it and pulled the knob.

I laughed when it didn't open, "Of course it's locked." I said to myself before coming up with the idea to find the key. I walked to the front and looked out the window to make sure Celeste wasn't back and then I went snooping. I started in the kitchen, going through the cabinet's and drawers, making sure to put things back in its place. I searched for a few minutes, but I didn't find any key.

Once I finished in the kitchen, I went into the living room. I checked the drawers on the end table and the jars that lined the fireplace, but there was still no key. I looked over in the corner of the living room where the bookcase stood. On the second to top shelf, in between the books, sat a wide bowl. I smiled when I saw something that looked like a key sticking out. I walked over to the shelf and looked up.

"I can reach that," I said to myself as I tried to stand on my tippy toes. A defeated sigh escaped my lips when I noticed I was still a few inches off. "Come on Alana," I motivated while leaning more against the case, putting my hand on the shelf in front of me to push up a little more. "Almost there," I grunted while stretching my arm as far as I could.

The bookshelf began to lean back against my weight. I didn't want to break anything, so I quickly let go and stepped back. The old case rocked back and forward a little, causing a medium size book on the middle shelf to slide forward out of its spot. I was getting ready to push it back, but curiosity got the best of me, so I grabbed it.

I flipped the book around and wiped the dust off the front of it. I noticed it was a type of photo album. On the front was a picture of twin baby girls. I opened it up and began to flip through the pages. The first page read Celeste and Celine Hill, which blew my mind. I always thought this place was called Hill house because it was built on a hill. But seeing this leads me to think otherwise.

I continued to flip through the old plastic covered pictures, smiling as the two girls grew older with each page. I couldn't believe this was Celeste and I couldn't believe she never mentioned she had a twin. When I got to the last page, I was surprised to see a newspaper clipping of the girls, standing in front of the Covington

Asylum. Both were wearing the oddly green colored uniform that all patients wear, and it was dated August 2000.

"August 2000?" I questioned while thinking back to the picture of Spencer and Celeste on their wedding day. "Wow, she was in an asylum a month before they got married."

I scanned the paper quickly and was surprised to see that they were admitted because of their Grandma being pushed to her death. They blamed each other and their mother didn't know who to believe so she sent them both to get help.

"Wow," I mumbled in disbelief as I took my phone out of my pocket and snapped a quick picture of the article. I closed the book and put it back on the shelf and then started to pace the floor. "What the entire hell is going on?" I spoke aloud to myself as I tried to think of ways this could have made sense, finally settling on my own theory. "Maybe Celeste's sister was found guilty, and once Celeste came home, she got married. Yeah, that makes sense." I said hesitantly, trying to really convince myself.

Dink...dink...dink

I spun around quickly, startled by the strange sound. Pausing for a second, I waited to see if I heard it again.

Dink...dink...dink

"What the hell," I said as I ran up the stairs, two at a time, to check on Spencer. I opened the door and he was still out cold. I checked the time on the phone, it was going on three-thirty. "How is he still sleep?"

Dink...dink...dink

There it is again, I thought as I left the doorway and headed back down the stairs, following the noise. It sounded like the pipes were clacking together. I slowly walked into the kitchen, looking around. I walked over to the sink and waited to hear the sound again.

Dink...dink...dink

I heard it again, but this time the clanging was further apart. My eyes slowly focused on the basement door. Could the sound be coming from there? I wondered as I walked closer, put my ear to the door and waited a few seconds for the noise.

"What are you doing?" Celeste's voice startled me, causing me to jump a little. I really didn't hear her come in.

"Oh my God Celeste, you scared me." I shrieked, while holding my chest.

"What are you doing?" She repeated in a sterner tone.

"Oh, I was hearing this weird banging noise, it sounded like it was coming from downstairs." I replied and she came more into the kitchen and listened as well.

Dink…dink…dink

The sound rang out, relieving me because I didn't want to seem crazy. "See, I've been hearing it for about ten minutes."

"Those are just the pipes honey." She said as she grabbed my arm and quickly led me out of the kitchen. "My dear Alana, I am extremely tired and would like to take a nap." She said while helping me grab my belongings, her weird pleasant voice had returned and the way she was talking was creeping me out.

"Oh, ok." I replied as she shoved my belongings in my arms and led me to the door. "You sure you don't want me to stay a while just in case Spencer wakes up? I can tend to him while you rest." I suggested as she opened the door and gently shoved me out of the house. I turned around to face her.

"He won't be waking up." Her dull tone struck me a little odd. "Have a great day honey, see you Monday." She said before closing the door in my face.

"Well damn," I muttered as I got a better hold of my things and headed to the car. Something just isn't sitting right with me. I thought as I threw my things in the passenger seat and got settled in the car. This whole situation just seemed off from start to finish.

133

I thought about everything I had seen today. From Celeste coming out of the cellar, to the article of her and her sister. Something was up, but what?

I pulled out my phone and pulled up the picture. My curiosity was taking over, and I really wanted answers to my questions. I glanced at the year again, my mother was working at the Asylum at that time. Thoughts quickly flooded my head, maybe I could go up there and show her the picture. Hell, she barely remembers me. How in the hell is she going to remember some damn twins from 19 years ago?

I sat in the car, debating with myself for a few minutes before finally deciding to make the trip to the nursing home. I hadn't been to see my mother in a while, so it wouldn't be a wasted trip. I started the car and took one last look at Hill house before backing out and descending the hill.

The nursing home was only thirty minutes away from Hill house. Most of the time was just getting down the hill itself. I pulled into the parking lot around four-fifteen. Turning off the engine, I contemplated on if I should go in or not. Being in front of this building was causing my stomach to do flips. I had to take deep breaths to keep my anxiety from spreading.

My mind wandered to the last time I had visited my mother. I remember it being extremely sunny out. I brought her breakfast and we sat outside on the patio to eat it. She was telling me stories about when she was younger, stories I had never heard before. I could tell the memory exercises had been helping and her mind was slowly coming back.

I was getting her back settled in her room when my phone rang. I went to my car to take the call. I was only gone about twenty minutes. But when I returned, I was met with a face full of confusion. I called her name and she gave me the most unfamiliar stare. It hurt me to my soul, to see that she had forgotten who I was. I spent the rest of the day trying to remind her, but by the end of the night, I was a stranger in her eyes.

"Damn," I cried out. "What's worse than forgetting your own daughter?" I instantly regretted the words as they slipped from my lips. "Really Alana?" I said, checking myself and my ill thoughts. It was not my mother's fault that she couldn't remember, and I had to stop making it seem like she can control what she knows and what she doesn't. I let out a deep sigh as the thoughts traveled around and around in my head. "That's it, I'm not going." I sighed and put the key back in the ignition.

I was getting ready to start the car, but a strong feeling washed over me. *Never be afraid to do the right thing.* My mother's sweet voice rang through my head and I couldn't help but smile.

"I can do this," I said, while taking another deep breath and exiting out of the car.

The sound of my feet hitting the damp pavement kept me focused as I quickly crossed the parking lot. I took in a breath of courage, headed into the building and walked right up to the desk. There, the receptionist greeted me with a big smile.

"I'm here to see Mrs. Bennet." I said while writing my name on the sign-in sheet. She gave me the information I needed, and I headed to the elevator.

I knocked lightly before walking into the average sized room. Some residents here had a roommate but thanks to mom's insurance she was able to have the room to herself. Mother was sitting in a chair and gazing out of the window. I swallowed the large gulp in my throat before finally speaking.

"Hey ma," I said in a soft tone.

"It looks like rain," she replied, gazing out of the window. I walked further into the room, glancing out of the window as well. The dark heavy clouds mirrored my feelings of heartache, and just like them, I to was seconds away from releasing.

Pulling up a chair, I called her name again. She looked up at me, and it took all my power to keep from crying. I could tell in her eyes that she still had no clue who I was.

"Ma, it's me Alana." I said while sitting down in the chair.

"Doctor, I've been looking into the patients charts and I really think we should stop testing. The serum is supposed to improve the memories, not take them away." She spoke, hesitantly.

"Ma, what are you talking about?"

"Doctor, the serum. It was created to help patients with memory loss. It's supposed to help them recover their thoughts with ease. But my studies show that not only are their memories not returning, but they are starting to forget their current memories as well. And at an alarming rate I might add." She continued to explain, but I had no clue what she was talking about.

I continued to listen to her ramble about the serum, which she called the CytoMNEM Inhibitor. It amazed me how she really was in the mindset of being back at work. It didn't surprise me though; she had spent most of her life in a hospital setting. And now she was permanently living in that same type of setting. Pulling out my phone, I figured this was the best time if any to show her the picture.

"Mom," I started off hesitantly as I opened the picture gallery. "Do you remember the Hill sisters?" I asked while showing her the article on my phone.

"Oh no, not that devil!" She said in a low growl. She pushed the phone away from her and started to shake her head. "Now that Celeste, she was sweet as pie, but that damn Celine, she had the devil tucked deep inside of her. And oh, could she hide it well, yes, she could. But I saw it, yes I did." She rambled in a hushed tone, before standing up and anxiously moved around the room.

I watched as she rummaged through her desk and drawers, obviously looking for something. I stood up and walked over to her. "Ma, what are you looking for?" I asked, but she seemed to not hear me as she continued to search. "Ma," I cried out and she looked over at me with bewilderment in her eyes. At that moment, I really thought she had recognized me.

"Doctor, here are my notes," She responded and handed me a tattered-up notebook. "Let me set up for the next patient." She continued and started to move around the room as if she was cleaning.

I looked at the notebook and realized it was one that I had given her when she first got admitted. I opened it up and flipped through the pages. It seemed to be more dreams then it was hospital notes, and the dates varied from months to years. I flipped through the pages until a certain one stood out to me. It was dated May 8th, which was the day she started to forget.

I was in the room with Mrs. Jones when the alarm sounded. I could feel a bit of fear rise inside of me as the code for riot was called over the intercom. I quickly jumped up and went into action. In the case of a riot, each staff member had a job to do. Mines were to make sure the north exit was locked.

I made sure Mrs. Jones was safe before I exited out of the room. I rushed down the hallway but stopped when I noticed the door to the medicine room was pushed open a little. This room was always locked, so I didn't understand why it was left open like this. I was about to close and lock it up when I heard some bottles clinking inside.

I slowly pushed the door open and stepped inside. I could see Nurse Linda, laying on the floor with blood spilling from her head. I could hear someone taking bottles of medicine out of the cabinets and throwing them inside of a bag. I noticed the cabinet; the resident was in was the one that contained the memory serum that Doctor Jamison had invented, and that serum could not get out of this building. First of all, it was not FDA approved and secondly, in the wrong hands this serum could be dangerous.

I glanced around the little room, trying to find something to defend myself with. Silently cursing as I knocked something over in the process. The patient stopped, causing me to hold my breath. My heart skipped as I waited to see who I was dealing with. A lump formed in my throat when I saw the sinister face. It was Celine, a resident that had been here for almost nineteen years. I could feel my body tense up as her eyes met mine.

Celine had a split personality disorder, and her alter ego had to have been made by Satan himself. I prayed silently, hoping that I was standing in front of the Celine I once loved. I asked her what she was doing and why she was taking the medicine. She said it was time for her to visit her sister and her husband. Her tone was harsh and aggressive, and I knew the visit she was planning was not going to be a happy one. I told her I couldn't let her do that and went to grab the bag from her hand.

That was the worst mistake I could have made. In that moment, I saw the change in her eyes go from light to sinister and before I knew it, she was shoving three syringes full of CytoMNEM into my hand. I couldn't believe how fast the medicine started to work as my memories began to fade away. The last thing I remember in that moment was my children and how hard it was going to be for them to see me like this.

I turned the page to see if she had written more, but she had not. I sat there reading and rereading her words in complete shock. I couldn't believe that Celeste's sister was the reason my mother memories had been erased, but now it all made sense. The reason the doctors could not pinpoint my mother's diagnosis was because it was caused by a man-made drug.

I stared at my mother as she moved confusingly around the room. I could barely keep up with all the thoughts that ran through my mind. This had happened months ago, and my mother clearly remembered it because she wrote it down. Maybe the drug was short time and it was finally passing through her system.

"Ma," I called out as I showed her the notebook. "Do you remember writing this?" I asked pointing to the page.

"May 8th, how can I have written that, and we are still in the month of Christmas? Do you still want mommy to buy you the Barney plush doll Lani?" She asked as she stared at the ground. "Oh my, I am getting so tired now." She continued and went to lay down in her bed.

"Hey Alana!" I heard a voice behind me. Turning around to see one of the health aides standing at the doorway. "It's been a while since I've seen you." She continued while walking into the room with a smile on her face.

"Yeah, I've been so busy between school and work. But now that school is over, I will be here more. How has she been, has she been remembering?"

"She has her days when she recalls. She does a lot of writing in her journal though. I'm surprise she brought it out. She usually keeps it hidden when she has visitors." She said while pointing to the book in my hand.

"Visitors?" I asked with a raised brow. "Who else comes to see her other than me and Duncan?"

"Her sister comes like twice a week." She said and I just stared at her.

"Sister? My mother does not have a sister." I replied hesitantly.

"Really? Because the lady comes here every week to see her. She's short, kind of heavyset and she talks with the sweetest voice." She continued and I still had no idea who she was talking about.

"Celine uses her sweet voice to hide her evil ways." My mother said with her eyes closed.

"No, the lady name isn't Celine, I think she said it was Celeste. But let me go grab the sign in sheet to make sure." She said before leaving the room.

I stood there in shock, trying to figure out what the hell was going on. "Ma," I said while walking over to the bed. "Do you remember what Celeste and Celine look like?" I asked, hoping she could make sense of it all.

"Oh, Celeste grew up to be such a beautiful lady. Still slim even though she eats like a football player," She said with a laugh. "I was so happy when she was able to leave the facility and marry that fine man of hers. Between me and you, I knew she didn't kill her grandma. She was way too sweet." She paused. "But that damn Celine, she could pretend to be the nicest person ever, but she has the devil in her." She repeated again.

"What does Celine look like now?" I asked hesitantly, as the gears in my head turned furiously.

"Celine use to be pretty just like her sister, but the medicine she took for her diagnosis turned her into this big manly looking thing." She said and I could feel my heart drop.

"Ma, let me see your arm?" I asked, knowing that the only reason Celeste would be coming to see my mother was to keep tabs on what she remembered. I grabbed her arm and pulled up her sleeve. Gasping when a red mark came into view. It was as if she had just been pricked with something. "Oh my God!" I shrieked. Not only was Celeste coming up here to see my mother, but she must have still been injecting her with the serum.

My heart started to beat a mile a minute as I ran out of the room. I pulled out my phone to call Duncan. "Pick up…. pick up…. pick up." I said in a panic as I walked out of the building and headed towards the car. He didn't pick up, so I hung up and called the station.

"Hello," I heard Duncan's voice say over the speaker.

"Bro I just left up here with mom and I found out the lady I work for has been coming here and drugging her. She's been making her forget her memories." I rushed.

"Wait, what are you talking about?" He asked in a confused tone.

"She has been posing as her twin sister and," I started say, but then paused. "Oh my God, Spencer! She must be erasing his memories as well. Bro I have to go back to Hill house." I said while jumping in the car.

"Hell naw, you bet not go back up there. If what you are telling me is true, then you need to let me handle it. Kaden and I were just about to head up to Hill House. That was the only clue we found at Scott's apartment. You stay there with mom and let me handle this." He responded and then quickly hung up the phone.

I stood in the parking lot, staring at the phone. It was going on five o clock. I knew it was going to take Duncan at least an hour to get there. But Spencer has no clue that his wife's twin has been erasing his memories. And now she has him sedated, there is no telling what she is going to do to him. I thought back to when Celeste, I mean Celine put me out of the house. The last thing she said was Spencer won't be waking up.

"Oh my God he could be in danger now." I shrieked, hopping into my car, I quickly pulled off into the direction of Hill house.

Chapter Four

Spencer

I tossed and turned as different versions of dreams raced through my mind. It was starting to feel like a cyclone, the same things playing over and over again. I couldn't place none of it, everything was just forming together into one big nightmare. I kept trying to wake up, but every time I opened my eyes I was back in another dream. I could not grab hold of reality and it was starting to make me nauseated.

My eyes shot open and I woke up in a cold sweat, gasping for air. It was dark, but I waited for my eyes to adjust. Once I got myself together, I pulled my notebook from out of my pillowcase, stacked the pillows so I could see and started to take note of the dream. I began the line with the date as always.

May 12th, 2019

I don't know how to explain this, but this dream didn't seem like a dream. It seemed like I was remembering a certain event, but at different times. All of them ending with Celeste standing over me with a twisted smile.

I continued to write, until I heard Celeste's croaky voice in the far distance. I put the pen down, closed my eyes and slowed down my breathing. I always did this when I wanted to focus on one sense.

"I don't know how much longer I can keep this up," she said to someone. When I didn't hear a reply, I figured she was on the phone. "He just showed up out of nowhere Charla, what was I supposed to do?" She continued in a fearful tone.

"Charla," I whispered to myself. "Where have I heard that name before?" I said while writing the name and the question mark inside of my notebook.

"...kill him," I caught the last bit of Celeste's sentence, and I quickly looked up. Did she just say kill him? I thought to myself, not sure if I had really heard it or not. "Spencer is ok, he's getting stronger though. I think the new aide is feeding him outside food." She continued to speak into the phone. "He hasn't showed any signs of remembering which is good, but," She paused, suddenly and I heard the floorboards squeak.

I didn't want to get caught, so I hid the notebook under the pillows and pretended to be sleep. I heard her open my door and step into the room. I laid there as still as a board, until I heard her step out of the room and close the door. There was an eerie silence, but then it was broken by her continuing her conversation.

"Sorry, I thought I heard something." Her voice was distant as if she had walked further away. "He's in the basement, it's soundproof, but I am going to go check on him." She said and I couldn't help but wonder who the hell was in the basement. "Yes, I go and see her every other day, she doesn't remember a thing."

That was the last thing I heard her say, as her footsteps descended. I quickly pulled out my notebook and took down these new details.

Something strange is going on here, and everything is not what it seems. I think Celeste is doing something to my memory. I don't know what she doesn't want me to remember, but now I think it has something to do with the person she is keeping in the basement. I don't know what is going on, but I have to get myself out of this bed and find out. Tonight, I am going to do the unthinkable. I am going to get up out this bed and try to walk. Celeste mentioned I am getting stronger. I feel like I've been in this bed longer than she is letting on. I don't even remember the last time I felt any pain in my leg or arm. If I was just in a car accident, I should be in constant pain. Something is off and tonight is the night I find out.

I skipped a line and decided to leave myself a little note before closing the book. I took a deep breath and decided to hide my secrets in a different place. Just in case something went wrong, I didn't want her to find it. I quickly stuffed it in between the mattress and slowly pulled myself up. My body was sore from laying in the same position, but I didn't let that stop me. I muffled a groan as I used my left hand to push my right leg out of the bed. It hit the floor with a heavy thud. I paused for a moment and listened, praying that she didn't hear me. Once I felt the coast was clear, I pulled my left leg over and out the bed as well.

I sat there for a few seconds, looking around for something to balance myself on. The only thing in reach was the dresser. I reached out with my left hand, but I needed to give myself a push. I rocked back and forth, while counting. On the third count I pushed myself forward and caught hold of the dresser, pulling myself up.

I stood there for a minute as a strong tingling sensation rushed down my leg. I clenched my eyes and mouth as tightly as I could to keep from yelling. The pain of my leg coming back to life was almost unbearable, but I got through it. Once the sensation stopped, I let go of the dresser and stood on my two feet, well my left foot and the cast. And to my surprise, I didn't feel any pain.

"Ok," I sighed to myself, but then tensed up when I heard soft breathing behind me. I slowly turned myself to the side, and there she was, Celeste, standing oddly in the doorway. The dim light casted a weird shadow over her face giving her this sinister look.

"Spencer, Spencer, Spencer." She said while shaking her head, disappointingly. "It is too early for you to be doing this. You are going to mess up your leg, sit down." Her pleasant tone, didn't usually creep me out, but tonight it made the hairs on the back of my neck stand up.

"Celeste, if I was just in a car accident a few days ago, how am I able to stand on a leg that's supposed to be broken?" I asked, while slowly turning my body all the way around to face her, my casted leg thumping the floor with each step.

"Spencer, you are pumped up on pain killers right now." She said, while pointing to the bottles of pills that lined the dresser.

I reached down and grabbed a bottle that was almost empty. "Celeste, this bottle is almost gone. I've only been here for a few days, right?" I asked, while shaking the bottle.

"No Spencer, you've been here for two weeks, you've only just started to remember the last few days." She said and I looked at her strangely.

"That is not what you told me." I argued.

"Yes, it is, the very first time you woke up, remember." She said patiently, still standing in the doorway. Her smile looking more ominous with each moment.

I faintly started to remember her saying something about being home for two weeks, but it seemed fuzzy. "No, that isn't right." I said while putting my hands over my head. Pain spread across my forehead as memories flooded my mind. I groaned deeply as I stumbled back against the dresser.

"Spencer, sit down." She said, sounding closer. I looked up and she had come further into the room. Her face seemed so strange as she smiled devilishly. Visions of her with this same menacing smile flashed through my mind and instantly a sense of fear rose through my body.

We stared at each other for what seemed like eternity. It was as if we both was waiting for the other to make the first move.

"Celeste," I started to say, but was startled when she lunched towards me. "Get back," I yelled as I pushed myself into action. I swung my casted arm, hitting her in the side while trying to keep my balance. She fell to the floor and I fell back against the dresser, knocking all the bottles down. After regaining my balance, I tried to run past her, but my casted leg slowed me down.

I was almost over her, but she grabbed the cast and made me fall forward into the arm of the recliner. My weight caused the chair to tip over, and I crashed to the floor with a hard thud. I felt a sharp pain in my left foot as if she had just stabbed me with something. I kicked back with my right foot and I felt it hit something hard.

I tried to scurry to my feet, but my body was going numb. My mind started to fade to black and I couldn't help but feel a sense of Déjà vu.

"Oh my God!" I shot up out of my sleep and looked around the room in a panic. It took me a second to notice the room was perfectly normal. I was in the bed, the bottles were still on the dresser and the chair was sitting up right. Was that really a dream, how could it have been so vivid?

The thoughts rolled around in my head as I caught a glance at Celeste's dry erase board. She had already changed the date and it read that today was May 10th. I took a deep breath and began to shake off my nerves. "I guess it was a dream." I said to myself, while remembering the date that I scribbled on the page. "Why am I dreaming about the future, I guess I am psychic now." I joked with myself, trying to lighten the mood.

Laying my head back on the pillow, I tried to relax, but I couldn't stop thinking about that dream. I couldn't help but shake the feeling, that it felt more like a memory. I looked at the board again and an uneasy feeling traveled up my spine. "No, there is no way." I said, shaking my head, trying to convince myself.

I looked around the room, trying to find something that could ease my mind, but everything seemed to be in order. Finally, I thought about the notebook and how in the dream I had stuffed it in between the mattress. Sitting up, I put my hand to the side of the bed and trailed my fingers along the edge. I took a deep breath to remind myself that nothing was there, but when I put my hands inside, I felt something weird.

I pulled my hand out and with it came not one, but two different notebooks. My heart began to beat a little louder as a familiar feeling began to wash over me. I opened one of the books and the first page was dated May 11th. I looked at the board again to make sure I hadn't made a mistake with the date, but the board still said the 10th. I sat in shock, reading my words, I didn't remember any of this.

I flipped through it and the last page ended on the 14th. I started to get an uneasy feeling in my gut. I scanned the page, most of it talked about someone named Alana and how she was helping me.

Maybe Celeste had forgotten to change the date this morning. My mind wandered as I tried to come up with any reasonable explanation that I could. I put the first notebook to the side and opened the second one. The first page was dated May 9th, I was writing as if I had just awakened. I was talking as if I had just met Alana, but in the other book I had been talking with her for days.

"What the hell," I muttered while looking at both notebooks. Had I maybe lost one and started a new one. My mind quickly dished out any plausible possibilities while trying to make sense of it all. But all of that was stopped when I flipped through the pages and landed on May 12th.

Celeste has been acting strange today. She was serving me breakfast and then stopped midway. I couldn't see her because she was standing at the dresser, but I could hear the tone of panic in her voice. I asked if she was ok, but she didn't respond. She just put the food in front of me and headed out of the room. I could eat it, but it looked like it had come from out of a dog's butt.

Even though this was not the moment, I couldn't help but laugh at the accuracies of the food. It did indeed look like a bunch of crap. Shaking my head, I continued to scan the page.

Lately I've been feeling a sense of déjà vu. I feel like I am stuck in some type of ground hog day movie. Just living the same day over and over again. I've been having these dreams, but a part of me is feeling like they are my realities. I am going to continue to play the role, just to see if this is real. I really feel like I am involved in some type of overzealous experiment.

Reading that line made me look back at the date. "What the hell is going on?" I mumbled, scanning the paper further.

Alana is here, looking very fine as usual. She told me that Celeste was outside gardening, but that sounded so strange to me. I have never heard her talk about gardening. Alana also gave me some peculiar information. She said that every time I started to remember, the next day I wake up not remembering anything. The statement confused me. At first thought, I figured it was a mistake on her part, but rereading my last entry her words spoke volume.

She told me to ask Celeste how many times I have forgotten, and I don't really know how I feel about that. I have a strange feeling that if I was to ask Celeste, all hell would break lose.

I scanned the rest of the page as all of these feelings I expressed through writing started to creep up the back of my neck. I flipped the page and was in complete shock when I noticed it was the exact entry from my dream. I skipped down, to the note that I had left myself, gasping in fear as I read my message.

Spencer, if you find this book and don't remember writing it, that is because Celeste is doing something to your memory. The first chance you get, get up and get out of there!

The air in the room suddenly became heavy, the sound of my heart pounded frantically through my chest. I tossed the book to the floor as I started to become queasy. I quickly gathered myself and inched towards the end of the bed. I didn't know where I was going, but I knew I had to make moves as quickly as possible.

I slowly put my casted leg on the floor, being careful not to make a loud thud. At this point I really had no real clue of what day it was, so I didn't know if Celeste was home or if Alana was here. Once I was sitting with both legs on the floor, I rocked back and forth until I had enough momentum to catch the dresser. Standing up right so quickly caused my head to spin and I suddenly felt sick.

Taking a deep breath, I tried to gain my composure. But I quickly got myself together when I caught a glimpse outside of the window. I could see Celeste standing in the yard, between the house and the shed. I quickly ducked down before she could see me. The pill bottles caught my attention. None of them were prescribed to me. Each bottle had a different person's name on it. I couldn't believe my eyes.

I waited a few seconds before taking a quick peek. Her back was facing me as she walked towards the shed. I looked further and I could see she had the cellar doors opened. I couldn't help but wonder who she had down there, but I was also not crazy enough to find out. I had to save myself first. Crazy thoughts rushed through my head as I eased my way towards the door and out of the room.

I got to the hallway and was surprised to see how big the house actually was. I went to walk down the stairs, but I couldn't see them because of the bandages. "I have to get down there." I said as I went to make the first step, stopping in my tracks when I heard a low voice talking in the distance.

I turned my head to the right and noticed a room with the door slightly ajar. The room was dark except for a little light that was coming from the tv. I listened closely, that is where the voices were coming from.

"Spencer, get that camera out of my face." I heard a woman say, followed by laughs and giggles. Instantly spiking my curiosity.

I looked at the front door and I knew that if I started now, I would make it out of here without getting caught.

"Come on Celeste, show me that little baby bump." I heard a male voice respond back. Assuming it was mine, I knew I had to at least check it out. I backed away from the stairs and slowly stumbled into the room. There was an old video playing on the tv and it was dated August 2001. I was amazed at how beautiful Celeste was as she showed off her bulging belly.

"Give me this," Tv Celeste said as she grabbed the camera and turned it around. "Now you say something," she added, showing a wide smiling Spencer in the frame. I stared at the man as he talked. Hating the fact that I didn't recognize him. I had had these bandages on my face for so long that I had no clue what I looked like as of now.

I unconsciously switched on the light and stumbled over to the dresser. I looked down and noticed a bunch of knocked over medicine bottles and a few syringes. I grabbed one of the empty glass bottles.

"CytoMNEM," I read once the label was in eyesight. Visions of her standing over me started to rush threw my head, causing me to drop the bottle. It landed on the floor with a sharp clink.

I tried to look for it, but of course the bandages were in my way. I looked at myself in the mirror and realized if I wanted to have any fighting chance, I would have to remove these restrictions.

I reached behind my head until I felt the flap that kept the bandages together. I pulled it open and started to slowly unwrap myself. My nervousness turned into anticipation as each layer became thinner and thinner.

Finally getting to the last layer, I let the bandages fall to the floor. I stood with wide eyes as the mirror revealed the surprise of my life.

Celeste

I watched as Alana pulled off and headed down the hill, before heading back into the kitchen. I reached on top of the refrigerator and grabbed the key to the basement, unlocked the door and headed down the stairs. When I got down there the deputy was laying on his stomach, using his badge to hit against the pipes. I rushed over to him, pulled him on his back and stared at his bruised face.

"Stop it!" I muttered in a low voice. "Stop it, before you bring her out." I said while snatching the badge from his grasp. "She's never happy when she comes out." I continued, speaking about my darker side. It had been a lot harder to control her, especially since I had taken the last pill a few days ago. I was trying to keep hold of the reins, but I was slowly losing control.

"You are nuts." The deputy's hoarse voice pulled me out of my thoughts. For a minute I had forgotten all about him. At this point I wished he could just disappear. He had been here for a few days and I had no clue what to do with him. It took all my might to keep her from killing him.

"You are going to have to kill him." The pleasant voice escaped my lips, startling me.

"Go Away!" I yelled, while trying to shake her out of my head. I couldn't let her get in control, I had to stay strong. The last time she took full control, the outcome was horrible. She continued to say awful things and started showing me visions of killing the deputy, but I didn't want to give in.

I grabbed my head and ran up the stairs and into my room. "Stop it…stop it…stop it." I yelled, pacing back and forth before running to the dresser and frantically looking for any type of pill to keep her calm. I contemplated shooting myself up with the memory serum, but quickly decided against it.

I looked at myself in the mirror and there she was, staring at me with her eerie smile. "Stop fighting me." Her voice flowed through my mouth again. I quickly turned away from the mirror and rushed over to the tv. Turning it on, I pushed an old cassette into the VCR and waited for the playback. A video of me and my twin sister popped on the screen. We had to have been no older than eight as we played on the swing set. I didn't know why but seeing us this happy always seemed to calm my nerves. I guess it reminded me of a simpler time, back before the darkness started to take over.

I sat down on the bed and stared dreamingly at the tv. I could feel myself falling into a daze as visions of the past flashed through my mind.

"Mom, why do we have to leave?" I whined, while following my mother around the house.

*"Celine, your grandma is doing better, and the summer is over. We have to get back home so you and your sister can start school."
She replied as she continued to pack her suitcase.*

"But mom we can go to school here." I cried, but it fell on deaf ears. "Please mom." I pleaded.

"No Celine!" She yelled, finally having enough of my antics. "Now go pack, we are leaving in the morning."

"This isn't fair," I yelled while stomping out of the room and locking myself in the bathroom. I paced the floor trying to calm my nerves, but I was so angry. I had finally found someone who liked me for me, and my mother was ruining it.

I collapsed to the floor and laid my head on the tub. Tears running from my eyes as the real reason I wanted to stay popped in my head. Spencer was my little secret. He was the only person that has ever chosen me and not Celeste. Everyone always loved Celeste because she was the 'pretty twin'. I was the outcast. There is no life for me back home, Spencer said he wanted to spend the rest of his life with me and we made sweet passionate love. And now I have to leave him.

"You don't have to leave." I heard a faint voice behind me, but when I turned around no one was there.

"Now I am going crazy," I cried while wiping my eyes.

"You just have to find a reason to make your mother stay." The eerie voice rang out again, this time startling me to my feet.

"Hello, whose there." I said nervously as I looked around the small bathroom. My eyes falling on the closed shower curtain. "Haha Celeste, very funny. Come out of there." I hesitated, waiting for her to pop out. "Celeste," I called out, this time pulling the curtain open. Revealing an empty tub. "Get it together Celine." I muttered to myself while walking to the sink.

I turned on the faucet, filled my hands with water and rinsed my face. I caught a glance of myself in the mirror and I could feel my heart drop. My reflection scared me so much that I stumbled back and fell into the tub.

"Don't be scared," I heard the voice say again, but this time I noticed my mouth was moving.

"What, what's going on." I shuddered, while pulling myself out of the tub.

"Your passionate anger created me, and I am here to help you with your problem." Her pleasant voice was comforting, almost mothering.

"How?" I asked, peering into the mirror.

"I know how much you love Spencer; you guys are perfect for each other. I am going to give your mother a reason to stay here in Hill house." She replied with a strange smile. "If you want me to?"

"Yes, yes I want you to do whatever you can. Just let me know what you need from me." I said in an excited but hushed tone.

"All I need for you is to let me in." She grinned while staring deeply into my eyes. A cold feeling rushed through my body and I started to fill up with doubt.

I was about to deny her request when I was startled by the bathroom door bursting open. "Are you in here talking to yourself," Celeste's voice rang out. "You are such a nerd." She continued as she moved closer to the mirror.

"No!" I yelled, stopping her in her tracks. I didn't want her to see my reflection, but when I looked back at the mirror, she was gone. It was just me looking back at myself.

"You're weird," She said as she reached on the sink to grab her hairbrush. "I can't wait to get home and back to my real friends." She concluded with rolled eyes and then left out of the bathroom.

I looked back in the mirror, my heart pounding with anger as I opened my mouth. "Use me," was the last thing I said.

I opened my eyes and was met with a pounding headache. I looked around, confused on how I had gotten to the top of the stairs. Celeste came running out of the room with horror in her eyes.

"What happened, what was that noise?" She asked and I stood there still in a confused shock. My mother's blood shattering scream pulled me out of my daze and both me and my sister leaned forward and peaked over the banister.

"What did you do?" My mother yelled at us as my grandma's broken body came into view. Blood leaked from her head as her face stared lifelessly up at us. "What happened?" She screamed up at us and we both looked at each other.

The next couple of weeks after that were crazy, especially when the coroner's office announced that our grandmother was pushed. Celeste put the blame on me, and I put the blame on her. Our mother was so distraught that she ended up placing both of us in the asylum. In her mind if she didn't know which one of us was crazy enough to kill her mother than both of us had to go. I guess she figured the counselors at the asylum could voodoo mind trick us into telling the truth.

My blackouts started more and more while I was in the asylum. I kept asking my reflection to stop, but I had already given her permission to use me and use me she did. I tried to prove to the doctors that my reflection was real, but she never showed up when

I needed her to. They eventually diagnosed me with a split personality and my sister was sent home.

My mother and sister stayed in town so they could visit every day. But as the time passed the visits came less and less. Until finally, they stopped coming all together. I received a letter on the day they were supposed to come. It was from Celeste. She spoke about the last time we met and how she didn't like the way I talked and threatened her.

I tried to remember what she was talking about, but I couldn't. It wasn't until she talked about how the nice voice I used while I was talking, scared mom. That was when I knew she hadn't met with me but had met with my reflection.

I stood in my room at the asylum, staring in the mirror. "Why did you do this?" I cried, waiting for my reflection to speak back. "Where are you?" I cringed as she made her appearance. Standing tall, with her hands folded in front of her. She was grinning, she was always grinning. "Why did you do this to me?

"I said that I will give your mother a reason to stay in Hill House and I did." She reminded and I gave her an angry glare.

"No, the reason was because of Spencer, now he isn't answering my damn calls anymore." I snapped and she stopped smiling.

"Oh no, we do not use that kind of language here." She said, making me even more upset.

"This is my life I can say whatever I want." I yelled and then proceeded to say every curse word in the book. I watched as her usual pleasant face turn vicious, and next thing I knew my hand was around my neck.

I tried to pry it from around my neck with my other hand, but the grip was to strong. I looked in the mirror and my reflection was smiling. Her hand wrapped around her neck as well. I could feel myself getting lightheaded, I had to do something to stop her.

Thinking quick, I pushed my body into the door as hard as I could and repeated it until I got Nurse Bennett's attention. She came rushing to the door and removed my hand from my neck.

"Celeste what are you doing?" She asked in a panic.

"It wasn't me; it was my reflection." I panted as my lungs filled with air.

"We are going to make sure your reflection never hurts you again," She responded with her arms around me. I couldn't help but cry as she rocked and comforted me.

Six years passed before the doctors were confident that I could regulate my diagnosis. My last episode was a year ago and even then, I was able to control the things my reflection could do. I couldn't have done it without the help of Nurse Bennett, she was there with me every step of the way. Honestly, she was more like a *mother to me then my own. She was the reason I was going home today.*

"Celine, I am going to miss you around here." Nurse B sighed as she helped me pack up my room. "Are you sure you don't want to stay for another week?" She joked while giving me the side eye.

"And miss out on my mother's homecooked dinner, no way." I chuckled, while zipping up my bag and swinging it onto my back.

"Is she and Celeste coming to pick you up?" She questioned, as we walked out of the room and down the hall to the lobby.

"No, I decided to take a cab." I paused when I saw the look on her face. "Nurse B, they know I am coming I promise." I said, even though it was a lie. I called the numbers that I had for them, but they were both disconnected.

"Ok Celine." She replied a little weary.

"Don't worry about me. I promise when I get settled in, I will come visit you. I would love to meet Duncan and little Alana." I added with a smile.

She smiled back. "Ok Celine," she paused as we stood in front of the door. "Come here," she said and pulled me into a hug. "You do good out there ok."

"I will, especially if I can run into Spencer." I said with a chuckle.

"I am sure he will be happy to see you." She smiled while holding me by my shoulders and looking me over. "I am proud of the woman you have become." She continued with tears in her eyes.

"Nurse B don't start; you are going to make me cry." I replied, while wiping my eyes.

"Ok, I am sorry." She said, letting me go. "Please say hello to your family for me." She added while pushing open the doors.

"Will do." I replied before heading out the door and getting into the cab.

I was nervous the whole ride up the hill. I couldn't wait to see my family; I had missed them so much. I wasn't mad at them for abandoning me, I completely understood. My reflection scared me, so I know when she appeared for them it had to be eerie.

"Wow, it seems bigger than I remember." I stammered as Hill House came into view. "Hey, can you pull over here." I asked the cab driver and he pulled over to the side. I really didn't want them to see me coming. "Here you go, thank you." I said to the driver as I paid the fair.

"Are you sure you are ok with walking?" He asked and I nodded my head before ascending the rest of the hill.

I climbed up the last stair, stood in front of the door and made myself presentable. "Ok Celine, big smile." I said and then rang the doorbell. I waited for a few seconds, before the door swung open.

"Mommy?" I heard a confused little voice and I looked down to see a beautiful little girl standing in the doorway.

"Alyssa, you know you are not supposed to open the door," I heard a male voice say and then was shocked to see who it was.

"Spencer?" I asked uncertainly.

He stood in shock for a moment, as if he had seen a ghost. "Celeste," he called out before shooing Alyssa away. "Go play in your room honey... Celeste!" He yelled out again as I stood there confused.

"What's wrong?" My sister's voice rang out in panic as she walked up. He nodded to me and her eyes widened. "Celine," she said in a low whisper. "Celine!" she repeated, but this time in a high squeal. "My beautiful sister." She continued as she pulled me into a hug.

I slightly hugged her back as I stared at Spencer and the ring on his finger. He barely made any eye contact as my sister pulled me inside. "Are you two married?" I asked as she pulled me into the living room.

"Yes, I met Spencer right after I came home from the Asylum. He approached me at my locker, it was love at first sight. He really

168

helped me get through losing you and grandma. We became so close that we got married that next month." She said while flashing her ring. "I got pregnant a few months later and boom, my own little family." She said with glee and I gave her the biggest smile I could, even though I was beyond devastated.

"Wow sis, that sounds like a dream." I replied while looking at Spencer. He continued to not make eye contact with me. "Where's mom?" I asked looking around the house, it had barely changed through the years, just a few new nick nacks here and there.

"Oh Celine," she said with a heavy sigh. "Mom passed away a few months ago, she had gotten very sick."

"What, why didn't anyone tell me?" I said with a raised voice.

"Mom didn't want you to worry, we had talked to the doctors and they said you were doing good. She didn't want the weight of that information to cause you to relapse." She explained, but I couldn't help but feel upset.

"I can't believe you," I replied softly. "You guys really abandoned me."

"No Celine, we wanted to keep coming. You told us if we continued to come you were going to slit your throat. Mom was terrified. You weren't yourself and we could see it."

"That wasn't me," I replied in an understanding tone. "But that part of me is gone. She has no control over my life anymore."

"That's wonderful," She said and then pulled me into another big hug. "Oh my God Celine, I've missed you. We have so much catching up to do. Let me go get the guest room prepared. Oh my God we can sit up all night and talk. We can give each other's medis and pedis." She continued to ramble as she headed up the stairs.

Once she was out of ear's reach I glanced over at Spencer. "Wow, my sister?" I muttered. "After everything I told you, you started to date my sister." I continued in disbelief.

"No, it wasn't like that." He tried to explain, but I cut him off.

"You didn't tell her about us. I called you every day and you never answered. I needed you."

"No Celine, you needed help, how would it look if the captain of the basketball team was dating a murderer. I couldn't take that chance." He said and I just stared at him in shock.

"But you said you loved me." I replied in a saddened tone.

"And I thought I did, until I met Celeste. She really brought a better side out of me." He continued and I just nodded my head.

"You know what, this is fine. This is ok. I can handle this." I spoke more to myself than to him. "I was gone for six years and I

expected you to have moved on. I am happy for you and I just want to say thank you for helping my sister through that rough time in her life." I said through closed teeth.

Accepting my truth, was a part of my recovery. My reflection latched on to my emotions and I had to learn to keep them in check. I closed my eyes and took this newfound information and packed it into a little box in my mind. I labeled it as garbage and put it by my mental trash can. This was another exercise of my recovery. I took a deep breath and opened my eyes.

"Ok, everything is set up. Now let's get you something to eat." Celeste said as she came down the stairs and grabbed me by my arm.

Celeste and I talked and snacked on some lunch for about an hour. I couldn't believe how much I had missed out on.

"Wow Celeste, I am so happy you were able to go on with your life." I said in the most believing voice I could muster up.

"It would have been better if I would have had you by my side." She replied, while putting her hands around mine. "I promise you. I won't abandon you again."

"Mommy, can I go outside to play?" I heard little Alyssa's voice behind me.

"Yes dear, but first I want you to meet your Auntie Celine."
Celeste responded.

"Hi Celine, why do you look like my mommy?" She asked
curiously.

"Well little Alyssa I am your mothers twin sister." I replied while
squatting down to her level. "You remind me of us when we were
your age." I continued while moving her curly hair out of her face.

I heard Spencer clear his voice before he grabbed Alyssa. "Go
head outside and play sweetie." He said and then looked at
Celeste. "Honey, can I talk to you upstairs for a minute?" He
asked in a stern tone.

"Yeah, sure." She said and then looked at me. "I'll be right back."
She added before they both exited out of the kitchen.

I waited in the kitchen for a few seconds before getting up to go to
the downstairs bathroom. It was the bathroom right under the
main bedroom, and the vent led upstairs. I knew Spencer had
called her up to talk about me, so I decided to listen in. I stood on
the toilet and put my ear to the vent.

"Celeste are you crazy?" I heard Spencer say in a frustrated tone.

"Spencer, that is my sister. She is the only family I have left." She
cried.

"She is not your family; I am your family." He replied.

"Spencer I am not going to abandon her. I might have you, but I am all she has." She argued.

"If she stays, then me and Alyssa are leaving." He replied and I could hear the seriousness in his voice.

I could feel the anger rising inside of me. I couldn't believe he was saying those things to her. I waited to hear Celeste's response.

"Spencer, I can't tell her to leave." Her voice was low and sad.

"Don't worry, I'll do it." He replied and that was all I needed to hear.

My blood was boiling as I ran out of the bathroom and out of the house. I needed to get away and get my mind straight before I opened the door to the bad thing inside of me. I ran down the porch stairs and around back. There was an old well behind the shed where I use to go and clear my head.

I peered over the well, hoping to hear the running water that once calmed my nerves. But the well had run dry. I tried to take the conversation I overheard and put it in a box, but I couldn't keep it closed.

"Celine are you mad?" I heard the pleasant voice rang out and my head.

"No...no...no." I said in a panic. "I locked you away."

"No, you didn't lock me away, I just sat back and waited for the right moment. Is this the right moment Celine?" She asked and I shook my head.

"Get out of my head, get out of my head." I yelled and screamed with my eyes closed.

"Are you ok?" I heard Alyssa's sweet voice as she ran up to me.

"Get away from me baby, I am not well." I said to her as she got closer.

"Look at her, she was supposed to be your daughter, not your sisters. But no, Spencer had to forget about you." My reflection's voice grew louder in my head. "And now he wants your sister to forget about you. You are just going to have to kill him." She taunted.

"I don't want to kill him, I don't care." I screamed.

"Kill him.... kill him.... kill him." She screamed.

"Stop it." I yelled while holding my hand over my ears. I could feel myself start to panic as she appeared in my mind. Her poise stature and eerie smile, caused a sense of fear in my body. I watched as she reached out for me. "Don't touch me," I screamed as her hand gripped my arm. I pushed back with all my might, causing her to fall to the ground and laugh hysterically.

And then there was an eerie silence. Followed by a blood curling scream.

"Celine, what did you do?" I heard Celeste yell and I opened my eyes. "Alyssa baby can you hear me?" She yelled down the well and that's when it all came together. My reflection had tricked me into pushing my niece down the well. "Spencer call the ambulance. Alyssa, baby speak to me."

"Oh my God Celeste, I am sorry. It wasn't me." I cried as I ran to the well and peered over. I could feel myself getting sick as Alyssa's broken body came into view. Laying the same way grandma was six years ago. "Nooooo." I screamed before I felt a sharp pain across my face.

It was from Celeste; she had slapped me. "Shut up you crazy bitch!" She yelled as she hit me again, this time with a balled fist. She continued to curse at me, calling me every name in the book.

"Stop it Celeste, please." I pleaded while trying to block her angered swings, but she continued. I could feel myself losing control as the vision of my reflection grew stronger in my head. "Celeste, please stop." I begged one more time, fearing that in any minute I was going to do something that I would regret.

"You are not my sister; you are a demon and I hate you. I hate you, you stupid demon bitch." She yelled in anger. Hearing those words from her mouth shocked me so much that I stopped

blocking. My arms dropped to my side as I stared at her emotion filled face. She cursed at me again while sending a right hook straight to my jaw.

I fell to the ground and hit my head on something hard, knocking me unconscious for a few moments. But those few moments were all my reflection needed to take over.

For the first time, I was able to actually see the things my reflection was doing. She stood up and grabbed Celeste by the throat. Squeezing with all of her might. I screamed for her to stop, but she did not. Spencer ran over and tackled my controlled body to the ground. But my reflection stood up as if she had felt no pain. She was getting ready to attack Spencer, but something caused her to shake violently. When my body fell to the ground, I saw an officer with a stun gun.

Everything seemed like a blur after that. The last thing I remember was seeing Nurse B's horrified face as they wheeled me back into the asylum.

A few months passed as I sat back in my mind, watching my reflection and her evil actions. She caused such a frenzy at the asylum that the doctors just didn't know what to do. Nurse B kept trying to plead to me, she kept saying she knew I was still in there and all I needed to do was fight. And after watching my reflection beat another patient's face in for swearing, I decided it was time to get back in control.

It took another year or so before I finally got back in the driver seat of my own body. But by that time, I didn't know who I was. I could barely recognize myself as I stared in the mirror. My hair had fallen out and I had gained so much weight from the different medications and test. It was like I had transformed into an entirely different person. And what sucked the most was that even though I was in the driver's seat, my reflection stayed in the passenger, smiling insanely, waiting for her chance to drive again.

Years went by as I sat depressingly locked away in this building. I didn't have any friends, because everyone was scared of me. I tried to explain that my reflection was not in control anymore, but that just made things worst. Until I met my best friend Charla Givens, a young and vibrant nurse with a sinister side like me. She helped me gain control of my reflection. She would sneak me certain medicine that helped me switch seats with my reflection whenever I wanted. We would go around the asylum, creating mischief together and it was all fun until she got fired. We continued to stay in contact via letters, but it was not the same.

My reflection one the other hand was starting to get anxious. She had gotten another taste of freedom and she was not ready to stay in the passenger seat any longer. It had become a constant fight to keep her at bay. Holding her off was becoming mentally exhausting.

May 8th, 2019 was when everything went to hell. I was sitting in my room, eating my dinner when the night nurse delivered me two packages. The first one was from the courthouse. I had put in a request to be released, I was doing good with handling my diagnosis and I was ready to leave here and start my life. I slowly ripped through the paper and scanned the letter.

"Sorry to inform you that your request has been denied per family." I read aloud and I could feel my heart strain. I could not believe Celeste wouldn't let me be released. It had been almost thirteen years since the incident, and I had even sent her a letter stating I would leave town. Taking a deep breath to keep me from spazzing, I bawled up the paper and tossed it in the garbage.

I got excited when I noticed the next package was from Mable Magee, an alias name used by my bestie Charla. I was surprised to receive anything from her, especially since she was being investigated for killing some people off a dating app.

I pushed my bedside table to the side, quickly ripped through the orange package paper and revealed a book. I stared at it oddly, not understanding why she would send this to me, but as I observed the cover it all made sense.

"The Other Me by Celeste Powell." I read the cover to myself and then flipped it over to read the synopsis. My eyes widened as I noticed the book was about me. She had turned me into some type of evil villain. I could feel my blood began to boil as I flipped

through the pages of the book, reading lie after lie. How could my own sister sit here and profit on a life that wasn't even hers.

"First you deny my request and then you write this garbage." I yelled while standing up and tossing the book across the room. I paced back and forth, irritated with this newfound information.

"No, she wrote the book first and then she denied you." My reflection said, causing me to stop pacing and look at myself in the mirror. There she was. Smiling intensely.

"Go away, I don't have time for your damn crap today." I sneered and she shook her head.

"We don't use that kind of language here." She said and it instantly brought me back to that day by the well when Celeste was swearing and beating me. She had said the same thing to her. "Celine aren't you tired of fighting with me, we could be out here living such a great life. I could have been gotten you out of here."

"You are the reason I am in here." I yelled.

"TomAto...tomato." She said changing the 'a' sound in each word. I rolled my eyes and started to pace the room again. My anger rising with each step.

"I can't believe this sh-stuff." I started to swear but didn't want to get on my reflections bad side.

"But Celeste, I know at this point you want revenge. The love of your life screwed you over, your sister abandoned you and this place not only fired your friend, but also took nineteen years of your life. Do you really want to die here Celine?" The question caused me to stop in my tracks. I hadn't even thought of that being an option, but now with this book going around. I might not ever get out.

My mind raced as I began to pace again. I tried to think of any possible way to get out of this place. I mumbled back and forth with each step, and then suddenly I stopped. I realized my reflection had become quiet. I turned, faced her and clasped my hands politely in front of me. Smiling, she became me.

The rest of the night became a chaotic mess. Fires being started, security throats being slashed, and mental patients being let lose. I had never seen so much destruction started by one person.

My reflection.

And she was the smartest thing walking. She was on a mission and I could tell she had been planning this for years. Just sitting in that passenger seat, watching, planning, and waiting on this moment. She made sure I didn't take my night meds; she knew who had what key and what codes got us where. She even knew how to disable the cameras. The building had become her playground and she was having a ball.

We found ourselves in the medical room, grabbing different medicine bottles and shoving them inside of a bag. I watched as she grabbed as much of the drug CytoMNEM she could. I heard something fall and noticed that someone had entered the room. My reflection filled up a few syringes before putting the last of the medicine in the bag.

"Celine, what are you doing?" I heard a familiar voice ask and we turned around. It was Nurse B, she never worked nights and I couldn't understand why she was here.

"I have to pay my sister and her husband a visit." My reflection spoke in a voice I had never heard. So deep, so demonic that it spooked me.

"Just leave her alone, don't hurt her." I said to my reflection hoping she would respect my plea. I wanted to warn Nurse B, but my reflection stopped me from gaining control. I fought harder as my reflection grabbed Nurse B's arm. I even tried mouthing a silent run. But it was too late, my reflection was already sticking her with the needles. I cried as she fell to the floor. There was nothing I could do; my reflection was ready to do anything to complete her mission.

Her presence ignited fury down each hall as we made our exit. They wouldn't have time to look for us, they had enough problems on their hands. It was raining when we reached outside and the walk to the house was a complete blur.

181

All I remember is the pain I felt as I stood in the living room. My reflection smiling in the mirror as my sister and Spencer made love behind us.

Celeste's eyes caught mine and her sounds of pleasure became sounds of panic as my reflection entered attack mode. At first, I thought it was funny seeing the look of fear on their face, but when I realized my reflection was causing more than fear I tried to stop her.

"Enough... enough." I yelled, but my cries were ignored. I was no longer in control. It felt as if she had tied me to the passenger seat, while she drove wildly down a killing spree way.

I closed my eyes, but the sounds of my sister's screams pierced my ears as my reflection stabbed her repeatedly. I tried to block out her pleas, but they rang loudly in my head. Spencer stood in shock, before making his run out of the house. My reflection jumped to her feet and took off after him.

Spencer's bare feet smacked the pavement as he ran nakedly down the stairs. He jumped off the third step and ran through the wet grass, slipping and sliding but not stopping. My reflection gained speed as she called out threats and taunted him. He rounded the back of the house and headed towards the dark wooded area that led down the hill.

Twisting and turning, the trees all looked the same as we went further into the darkness. Fear rose through my body as Spencer began to disappear. He couldn't get away, if he did, he would tell everyone.

My reflection stopped and looked around, both of us hoping to catch some glimpse of our target. The road was just up ahead, a set of headlights appeared in the distance. My reflection waited patiently; she knew Spencer was going to make a run for it. A stick snapped and Spencer appeared out of nowhere, running full speed ahead to the road. We took off after him.

I started to get nervous as he picked up speed. He was getting closer to the road, closer to his salvation. My heart started to pound as he reached the top and crossed over the railing. My refection got closer, but I knew right then and there, everything was over.

Suddenly, the unthinkable happened. Spencer ran into the middle of the street, waving his arms frantically. The car blew its horn and tried to stop, but it was too late, and Spencer's body went flying across the road.

I stared in shock as a truck that was behind the car, swerved and hit the side railing. I couldn't believe how much noise it made as it tumbled down the side. The little car that hit Spencer sped off down the highway. It was in that moment, my reflection let go of the reigns. Leaving me standing awkwardly, staring at this disastrous scene.

"No, don't leave me with this mess." I pleaded, while staring at dismembered body parts of Spencer laying on the ground. My heart began to race, I suddenly felt sick as visions of the night irrupted through my mind.

"Oh my God." My yells echoed through the night air, followed by the sounds of me emptying my stomach contents into the dark wet pavement. "How could I have let this happen; this was not me." I cried out, realizing that I never wanted it to go this far.

"Help," I heard someone call out. I ran to the side of the road and peered over the broken railing. I could see the truck and I noticed someone was moving inside. I quickly slipped over the railing and ran down to the wreckage.

"Help me, I think I broke my leg." He grunted and I felt so bad.

"Leave him." My reflection spoke. I ignored her, but I can still feel her watching me through the truck's cracked mirror.

I could tell he was badly hurt, by the way he was laying. Most trucks like that didn't have seatbelts. So, I know he had gotten tossed around. I called out to him, but he didn't reply.

"He must be unconscious." I said as I figured out a way to get him out.

"So, what are you going to do with him, become the new Celeste and Spencer? "My reflection taunted with a wicked laugh, planting a seed that she knew I would water.

I pulled him out of the truck and his phone fell out with him. I knew at this point I needed help, so I used his finger to unlock it. I called Charla and explained to her what was going on and she told me she was on her way to help. I hung up the phone and proceeded to drag this man back to the road.

"I'm not ready to die, " the accident victim said and tried to break away.

"Spencer I am trying to help you. " I said, hoping he was delirious from being unconscious. He didn't respond and when I looked down again, his eyes were closed.

His phone began to ring, causing me to drop him. I pulled the phone out of my pocket. It was Charla letting me know she was coming up the hill. I looked up as soon as she said it and saw the headlights. I told her to stop and was surprised to see she was in an ambulance. I didn't even ask her why, I just grabbed the body and pulled it back to the road.

"Stay with us, " I said to him as he opened and closed his eyes. He was losing blood and all I could do was pray. I didn't want another death on my hands, especially someone that didn't have nothing to do with anything.

"Celine, who is this?" The blue-eyed man with Charla asked as he worked on the accident victim.

"This is Spencer." I replied and Charla looked back at me from the driver seat.

"I thought Spencer got hit." She asked and I just sat there. Both her and the man looked at each other, but no one said anything.

We ended up in the shed where Charla's blue-eyed friend went to work on my new love.

"I'll be back." I said as I left out of the shed and quickly went back to the house. "Oh no, this won't do." I said while looking at my sister's lifeless body. Grabbing her by the arms, I slowly dragged her to the kitchen and sat her by the basement door.

I grabbed the key, unlocked it and kicked her body down the stairs. "Ok, now let's clean up." I said to myself as the spirit of a housewife took over my body. I had to make sure the house was nice before my husband came home.

The thought was weird, and I didn't know why I was thinking it. I caught a glimpse of my reflection and she was standing straight up with her hands clasped in front of her, smiling. Her actions suddenly became my own.

When I opened my eyes, I was back in the shed. It was as if I had never left. "Celine are you ok?" Charla's worried voice asked in the distance.

"Call me Celeste." I replied.

She stared at me for a few seconds, before realizing what was happening. "Ok, that's my girl, learn to adapt." She smiled before leading me over to the now casted up man.

"Will he live?" I asked while trailing my hand over his hard-shelled leg.

"It's hard to tell." Blue eyes replied.

"Charla, what does he mean?" I asked and he began to explain the injuries. "Saving Spencer is the only way." I said as we moved away from the sleeping body and started speaking low.

"But this isn't Spencer." He replied hesitantly. I pulled out a bottle of CytoMNEM and saw a hint of recognition in his eyes. "Oh, it's one of those parties." He said with a devilish grin and I knew we were all on the same page.

A loud crash startled us; it was my new husband trying to get up.

"Let me handle this." Blue eyes said while swiping the needled from my hand. A wild look danced across his eyes as he pinned down my beau's arm and erased his memories.

The night continued.

My last thoughts being of me, standing in front of the mirror with the syringe in my arms watching this beautiful stranger's face being wrapped up in my web of lies.

When I came to, I was standing in the doorway of my room, staring at the same stranger's face and looking just as confused as he was. I thought about the moments where I couldn't remember anything, and I finally realized. My reflection had been erasing my memories as well.

"Celeste, who am I?" The man said to me and I just stared at him. "Celeste, who am I?" He asked again while grabbing a picture of Spencer off the dresser. "Because I damn sure ain't this person." He yelled, startling me for a moment.

"I don't know what's going on." I stammered as I came closer into the room, catching a glimpse of my reflection. I stared at her as she stood smiling. "Have you been erasing my memories?" I asked her, but she continued to smile.

"What?" The stranger said as he looked behind him in the mirror. "Who are you talking to?"

I ignored him and still stared at my reflection, waiting for my answer.

"Celine, you are weak, I had to erase your memory. You were talking about going to the police and I wasn't going to be locked up again." My mouth moved as she spoke pleasantly through me.

"What the hell is going on?" The stranger yelled and then looked at me oddly.

"Oh no, we do not use that kind of language here." My reflection said as she kicked me out of the driver seat. I tried to get back in control, but the lack of medicine made her stronger. She stood with her back straight and her hands clasped down in front of her. She was smiling as always, and I could tell the stranger was getting uncomfortable. "Now Spencer, you are sick. Let's get back in bed."

"I am not Spencer." He replied.

"Well then, who are you?" She asked tauntingly.

"I am," He said and then paused. "I don't know who I am." He continued in a defeated tone. "Just take me back to my room."

Me and my reflection both stood in a surprised state. "Why are you giving up so easily?" She asked with raised brows.

Look at me," he said while pointing to his cast. "I can't move quickly; I can't fight you and I don't know who or where I am. I don't even want to hurt you. You've taken care of me and honestly." He paused before revealing his million-dollar smile. "I love you Celeste." He professed and I could feel my heart warm as I began to take control of my mind again. My reflection couldn't control happiness, only chaos. "I don't think I've ever been cared for like this, I don't think I've ever been this happy." He continued as he walked closer to me, reaching his hand out and caressing my chin.

My body began to melt as this tall, dark and handsome man stared down at me. He was so good-looking; despite the dryness his face was experiencing from being under the bandages for so long. His hair was braided, and his beard was shaped up so perfectly. Visions of me taking care of him began to flood my mind. I didn't remember shaving him and doing his hair, but my mind was telling me otherwise.

"Spencer," I started to say, but he placed his finger over my lips.

"Shhh..." he said as he leaned down to kiss me, causing my body to go into a complete vulnerable state. I closed my eyes and waited for his sweet lips to touch mine. But I never felt them, all I felt was his hand on my arm as he shoved me out of the way. It was all a ploy to get pass me and that made my body explode with anger.

I ran after him as he headed for the door. Jumping on his back, I knocked him off balance. Pushing him into the hallway, he fell to his knees as I hit him in his back.

"Get off me you crazy heifer." He yelled as he threw his body back, causing me to fly into the wall. He crawled closer to the stairs and stood up. I tried to attack him again, but he turned around and grabbed my neck with his free hand. He started to squeeze with all his might, which wasn't much, but enough to keep me subdued.

I tried to beat his arm, but he continued to squeeze. Visions of my life started to push through my mind as my breathing quickened. I could feel myself becoming lightheaded, but right before my body shut down, a loud scream rang through the air.

It must have startled the stranger because he let me go and looked around in a panic. I took that as my chance. I used all the might I had and pushed into him. He was standing in front of the stairs and that shift in balanced caused him to tumble down. I rubbed my neck and tried to catch my breath.

I didn't hear any movement after that. When I looked down the stairs. The stranger was awkwardly spiraled across the floor. Unconscious.

Chapter Five

Alana

I decided to take the back way up to Hill House. I didn't want
Celine to see me coming. My mind ran crazy as I ascended the hill
as fast as I could. It had started to drizzle, and I didn't want to spin
off the road. The real Celeste must have been trapped in the
basement. That's the only thing that could explain Celine carrying
the buckets from the cellar to the shed.

"Oh my God! The banging I heard today must have been Celeste
trying to get help." I yelled aloud, as the realization set it. "I can't
believe I just left without doing any further investigations."

Just the thought of someone being trapped in the basement made
me increase my speed. I was so focused on driving that I almost
missed the squad car that was parked on the side of the road.

"Damn how did Duncan beat me up the hill." I asked myself
before breathing a sigh of relief. Apart of me was a little scare to
venture in the house alone. I passed the car and continued. Pulling
around back, I cut the engine and got out of the car. When I walked
around the side, I noticed the cellar was open. My heart quickened
as I hid myself. I peeked, trying to make sure Celine wasn't
around.

When the coast seemed clear enough, I gathered my nerve and quickly ran to the cellar. Slowly I walked down the stairs, making as little noise as possible. There was a musty, decaying odor in the air. The kind you would smell if you had a dead mouse, trapped behind a wall. I started to get nervous, especially since it was dark as night down there.

The smell was getting stronger as I reached the last step. I pulled my cell phone out of my pocket and turned on the flashlight. The little stream of light danced across the floor as my hand shook anxiously. I was scared. I couldn't help but wish that I was still waiting at the nursing home with my mother. What was I thinking?

"Hello," I called out while moving the light around the room. "Celeste are you here?" I asked but there was no response. I thought I heard some movement to the left of me, so I quickly turned and flashed the light. "Celeste?" I called out as I noticed a woman sitting next to the wall, with her head laid against it. "Oh my God Celeste," I said as I rushed over to her and grabbed her shoulder.

I almost threw up when the woman's head tilted back and revealed a decomposing stare. I jumped up and stumbled back trying to keep my composure. Suddenly I felt something touch my leg. I let out a loud scream and shun the light towards the ground.

There was a hand wrapped around my ankle and I recognized the tattoo on the wrist. "Scott?" I gasped while bending down to help him. He was bruised and bloody as if he was just beat. I cursed when I noticed he was locked up. Looking around, I noticed the door leading to the kitchen was open. "I am going to find the key." I said as I gave him the cell phone for some light. I quickly turned away, seeing him like this hurt my heart. But even though I was terrified, I knew I had to help him and Spencer.

Taking a deep breath, I made my way up the old wooden staircase, one foot at a time. The second to last step began to creak. I stopped. Holding my breath, I listened to the silence. Please Lord be with me, I prayed while stepping over that stair and up to the door.

I continued to pray in my head as I peered around the corner. The house was always quiet. But in this moment, it was an unnervingly, eerie silence. I had to prepare myself for anything. I took another deep breath and quietly pushed on into the living room.

"Spencer," I blurted as his fallen body came into view. He had a blanket over his face, and he wasn't moving. I nervously bent forward, fearful of seeing another dead body. "Spencer." I called out in a low whisper, while slowly pulling the blanket off his face.

I stood up in shock as this unfamiliar face came into view. This was not the man in the pictures. And this man did not have any scarring from the laceration Celeste told me about. This man was not Spencer.

His eyes opened and panic ran across his face. "Alana, watch out!" He yelled, causing me to duck. It was just in time because Celine was in the middle of swinging a bat. I turned around, looking at her with wide eyes. "Celeste did you really just try to hit me with a damn bat?" I blurted in disbelief, I couldn't even say the right name.

"What are you doing here Alana," She responded in her creepy pleasant voice.

"I am here to help Spencer and my friend you have locked in the basement." I answered sternly.

"This is after work hours. You are now trespassing and dare I say breaking and entering." She replied, while moving closer, dragging the bat behind her.

I stepped back, strategically thinking of my next move. She moved forward again, and I could tell she was trying to scare me. Little did she know I was more angrier than scared as the visions of my mother rushed through my head. She might have been better if this crazy hag wasn't putting that memory drug in her every week. "Did you know that my mother was Miranda Bennett?" I asked through gritted teeth.

"Nurse B is your mother," her voice was sweet, but I could tell she was taunting me. "I knew you looked kind of familiar. Especially now, you both have the same fear face." She said as she lifted the bat high into the air. The look of aggression on her face let me know she was ready and willing to end my life.

I knew at this point it was now or never. I took a deep breath, gathered all my fight and charged toward her. Knocking her down and causing the baseball bat to click and clack across the hardwood floor.

"You crazy heifer," I yelled while hitting her wildly. She tried to fight back but I had the upper hand. "You are the reason my life is in a disarray." I continued taking all my anger out on her face and body.

She smacked me in my face causing me to fall off her. She rolled on top of me and clutched her hand around my neck. I tried to claw her off, but she just gripped tighter.

"Stop," She said in her croaky voice and I could feel the grip getting lighter, but then tightening again. It was as if she was fighting with herself to let me go. "It wasn't me," she cried out. "I loved Nurse B and I would never hurt her." She said in her normal croaky voice. "I tried to stop my reflection from doing it, but I can't control her anymore."

"Shut up," the pleasant voice said and began to squeeze harder.

"Go," She yelled in her normal voice and I felt her hand completely let go of my neck. I scrambled to my feet and turned around. The door was right behind her and I wanted to run pass, but I couldn't leave Spencer or whoever he was. I ran to him and tried my hardest to get him to his feet.

"Alana, just go. You don't have that much time." He said as he struggled to get up. I looked back and Celine was using everything she had to keep her reflection at bay, but by the time we got ready to run, it was too late. Celine had lost hold and her reflection had taken over.

She stood in front of us, her face plastered with a devious grin. "I am going to kill you." She said in her pleasant tone. "I am going to kill both of you." She screamed louder as she charged full speed ahead.

Bang.

The shot rang through the air and a loud ringing noise filled my ears. I looked around frantically, trying to focus on what was happening. Celine stood frozen in front of us, her eyes filled with pain. She dropped to her knees and my eyes widened as she fell to the floor.

"Duncan?" I t as he rushed over to me with tears in his eyes.

"Alana, I thought I told you not to come here." He said as he pulled me into a hug.

"I'm sorry bro." I replied while looking down at Celine. She was laying on the floor, staring up at me. She was breathing hard and I could tell she was fighting for her life. She kept repeating the words, 'I am going to kill your ass.' Her tone was not pleasant anymore but was harsh and cold. Her voice was getting lower and lower, but she continued to say those words.

I bent down to her level and looked right into her eyes as her life slowly faded away. "Duncan, how did you know I was here?" I asked as I stood up and turned to face him.

"I called him." I heard a disgruntle voice from the kitchen, I looked over and saw Scott being helped out the basement. His arm was around Kaden's neck as they stumbled out of the kitchen.

"Well at least you found your brother," I said, noting the reunion.

"This man ain't my brother," Scott answered while holding his side.

"No, I am not his brother. I am just a person that owed his mother a favor." Kaden said with a hint of relief.

"I am sorry about your wife Mr. Powell." Duncan said as he helped the strange man over to where we were all standing.

"That wasn't my wife and I am not Spencer. I honestly don't know who I am." He replied with a sense of sadness.

"Jaxon?" I heard Kaden's voice as he moved closer to the stranger. "Jaxon is it really you." He said while holding the man by the shoulder. "It is you!" He continued while pulling Jaxon into a hug. "Bruh, I've been trying to find you for two months."

"Two months?" The guy he called Jaxon said in a confused tone.

"I knew something wasn't right when you didn't pick your car up." Kaden continued but Jaxon just stared blankly at him. "Jax, wassup man, don't you recognize me?"

"I don't remember anything about my past, I think Celeste has been drugging me." He said while looking at the lifeless body on the floor.

"That isn't Celeste, that's her twin sister Celine. Celeste's body is in the basement, looks like she's been dead for a few months." I replied and my brother looked up at me.

"This is crazy," he replied while shaking his head.

"Man, I told you there was a missing person in this town." Scott grunted as he walked closer to me. "I just didn't know you was going to lead me to him." He flirted with a sly smile.

I was about to respond, but I was cut off. "I am going to kill you bitch!" Celine yelled while grabbing me by my ankles.

"Oh no, we don't use that kind of language here." Jaxon said while stomping down on her hand with his casted leg. She screamed in pain, letting me go in the process.

"She's the patient that caused the riot at the asylum, do you think we should call them?" I recalled and we all looked at each other.

"Does she have any other family?" Duncan asked and I stared at him in disbelief.

"Duncan," I gasped but he didn't look at me.

"Does she?" He asked again, while looking at Jaxon.

"I don't know, I mean," he paused. "I have heard her talking to this woman named Charla."

"Charla," Scott said to himself with a certain look on his face. "I knew it! I knew this had something to do with the Tender Killer." Scott continued with a big smile on his face.

"Damn," Duncan said, and I could tell he was thinking of the right thing to do.

"It doesn't matter," Scott said as he stared down. All eyes fell on Celine as she took her last breath. We didn't have to do nothing, because it was already done.

"I am going to call the authorities in on this one." Duncan replied as he pulled out his phone and called this situation in.

"My brother's first month as sheriff and he has cracked his first case wide open. This is a cause for celebration. Shots on me." I said trying to ease the mood.

"The only shot I'm taking is a shot of morphine. I can barely see straight." Scott said as he fell forward into my arms.

"Come on, let's sit you down." I said while helping him to the couch.

"The big heads are on their way and they are sending an ambulance for you guys as well." Duncan said as he hung up the phone.

"Thank God." Jaxon sighed in relief. "But until then, can someone please help me get this cast off. I have an itch that I been trying to reach since this thing started." Jaxon said as he patted his leg frantically.

We all looked at him and then each other before letting out a loud hearty laugh. And boy did it feel good to laugh, especially after a day like this.

Epilogue
Kaden Bishop (Nice for What)

I was at the hotel packing up all my things when I heard the notification on my phone chime. It had been two days since being at Hill House and I still couldn't get the image of Celeste and Celine's dead bodies out of my head. I grabbed my phone and opened the message from Duncan.

Duncan: Hey can you meet me at the station in thirty minutes?

I glanced at the time, it was already twelve and I had a long drive ahead of me. But the station was in the direction I was going, so I replied with a short, ok. I put my phone in my pocket, finished packing and headed out of the small room.

After turning in my key, I put my belongings in the car and headed towards the station. "I hope Dunc is already there, the faster I can get out of this eerie town the better." I mumbled as I looked out the window at the scenery. It was pretty peaceful here, but I preferred the excitement of the city and plus I was missing my girl Riley and my daughter Kinsley.

I pulled up to the station about ten minutes later and headed inside. I didn't see Duncan, but I did see Daniel... well... Scott, sitting at his desk.

"Hey man." I said as I walked up to him.

"Hey," he said but I could tell he wanted to say something else.

"I haven't called your mother yet, if that's what you are worried about." I said, feeling the tension in the air. "But she will be calling me soon." I continued once he didn't respond. "Is there something you want me to tell her?"

He looked at me and I could tell he was thinking of something to say. He finally nodded his head and let out a loud sigh. "She was right man, she always told me I couldn't escape who I really am, and she was right. I have a savior complex and living in the city, I found myself getting into so much trouble because I was trying to help everyone. That's why I moved to this little town."

"Because you have a savior complex?" I asked, not really following what he was saying.

"Yeah, I figured a small town like this where everyone knew each other, less people would need help. I became a deputy just so I could satisfy myself a little bit. But it wasn't enough for me. That's why I was so excited when I found your friend's truck on the side of the road. I just knew there was a case that needed to be solved and a person that needed to be saved, but then I hit a dead end." He finished while shaking his head.

"How did you end up in the basement of the Hill House?"

"Trying to be a savior," he replied shaking his head. "Alana was telling me about Spencer and Celeste and it just didn't make sense.

So, I went there just to make sure she was in a safe environment, but when I saw that shed, I knew something was off." He paused and then shook his head in shame. "It was so careless of me to have gone to that house without help, but it was something about the danger of it that drew me in."

"Damn man." I replied while shaking my head.

He looked down on his desk and shuffled around some papers. "My mom is the same way, that's why she continues to save people who can't save themselves." He said and then gave me a certain look.

I looked away.

"Don't worry man, I am not here to judge you. I really just want to say thank you, you saved my life." He paused. "But how did you know where I was?"

"You sent an alert out to Ann's phone, it sent her your location." I replied and all he could do was laugh.

"Do you know my mother set this account up years ago. I can't believe it still had that information in it. I swear that ain't nothing but God looking out." He replied and I nodded my head in agreement.

"Hey you two." I heard Duncan's voice behind me.

"Wassup Dunc," Scott replied as he grabbed the papers he was working on and handed them to the sheriff. "The papers are done."

"Damn Scott, you really resigning?" Duncan said as he looked over the papers.

I looked at Scott with wide eyes. "You're not going to be a deputy anymore?" I replied, while glancing at the resignation papers.

"Naw man, I can't limit myself anymore. It's time for me to go back to the big city and try my hand at being a detective or something.

"Well, you definitely have the skill sets for it." Duncan noted and we all couldn't help but laugh.

It felt good to laugh with these guys. The only other guys in my life are forced on me by my girl and her friends. It was really going to feel good to have Jaxon back in action.

We continued to talk until we heard the doors to the station open.

"Hey guys." Alana gleamed as she walked into the station. "I made some cookies."

I couldn't help but feel a familiar type of way about her as she walked around the room. Her entire presence reminded me of...My thoughts trailed off as I looked up and saw Jaxon walking into the building. Seeing him now, was like seeing a ghost.

Jaxon Hudson (Nice For What)

I was already on my way to the station when Duncan called. I pulled in the parking lot and parked in the far back. I didn't want to be the first person to arrive and plus I really needed a quick nap.

I closed my eyes, but my mind wouldn't settle. The last two days had been hell. My dreams, my nightmares and my memories were all rushing my mind simultaneously. It still felt as if I was stuck in a time loop. "Two months." I grumbled to myself as visions of those days combined with each other. But my memories were even worst. Thinking about Darlina and the baby hurt me to my core.

I sat up and caught a glance of Kaden walking into the building. I still couldn't believe he was here to find me, it's as if this was a scene from an amazing thriller or something. I couldn't help but wonder what I should do next. Should I go back to the city and worry about seeing Lina, or worst Adrian. Or should I just stay out here like I originally planned.

"Oh snaps, my car." I blurted, remembering the money I had in the trunk. "That car is probably towed somewhere." I said in the same breath. I looked up again and saw Alana walking into the building.

Visions of my time with her danced in my head. It was always great to be in her presence, she was sweet, caring, funny and she could throw down in the kitchen. Thinking of her made me happy and I realized that she would be a great reason for me to stay. I waited a few more seconds before getting out of the car and heading into the building.

"Hey Spenc... I mean...er..um." Alana stammered. "I'm sorry." She continued while handing me a bag of cookies before dashing off, embarrassed.

"Thank you." I called after her and glanced over at Kaden who was giving me a sly smile.

"Good, everyone is all here." Duncan said with a clap. "I just wanted to check in with everyone, just to see how you all were doing." He asked and looked around the room. We all stood silent for a few seconds before answering at the same time. We all said we were ok, but we could all hear the uneasiness in each other's tone.

"Yeah, I feel the same way," He replied. "I know what we went through was crazy, but looking on the bright side, we all made it out alive. I can't even imagine being in that situation and I am happy that all of you guys are here. I found out that Celine had started a riot at the asylum and went on a killing spree. The woman down in the basement was indeed her twin sister and we have no idea what she did with the real Spencer." He said while looking over at me. "Thanks to all of your statements her death was ruled out as self-defense."

"Thank God." Alana said with a sigh of relief.

"Kaden, I want to say it was a pleasure working with you. You came here on a mission to find Scott and you did just that. You sure you don't want to stick around; I am in need of a new deputy." He joked, and I looked over at Scott.

"You're leaving?" Alana gasped and Scott nodded his head.

"Yeah, I have a meeting with the head of Phoenix PD. I have all the skills and certifications to become a big city cop." He said with a wide smile.

"I wish you all the luck," Duncan said and then glanced back at Kaden. "So, what do you say?" he persuaded with a nudge.

Kaden let out a small chuckle before politely declining. "Nah man, I have a fiancé and a baby girl back home. And after the last few days, I don't ever want to be away from them again." He paused and then looked at Jaxon. "You still trying to be my best man?"

"Oh, you mean to tell me, I haven't been replaced with Adrian?" I joked

Kaden's face went stale. "Man, please save me from that torture." He continued and we both let out a big laugh. Duncan started talking again, I glanced over at Alana and caught her staring at me. When she noticed I was looking she quickly looked away and I couldn't help but smile.

Once Duncan stopped his short speech, we all started to break off into smaller conversations. I figured this was the best time if any to catch a conversation with Alana, so I made my way over to her.

"Hey Alana, I'm Jaxon. Nice to meet you." I smiled, with my arm extended.

She looked at my hand and then trailed her way up to my face. A small smile creeped across her lips as she grabbed my hand. "It's nice to meet you as well." She paused and then pulled me into a hug. "Come here man, acting like we're strangers!" She continued as we embraced each other. I couldn't help but melt in her arms as her intoxicating scent filled my nostrils. She pulled back and looked me up and down.

"What?" I asked a little nervous.

"I just keep thinking about all those conversations we had. I can't believe it was you and not Spencer under those wraps." She said and we both kind of stood there in silence, not really knowing what to say.

"Well," I said while clearing my throat. "I know it may seem weird, thinking I was someone else. But at the end of the day whether I was Spencer or not, you still helped me. If it wasn't for you and your memory exercise, I would probably still be laying in that bed, lost. The doctors said being able to write down my day to day memories is what helped my mind fight off the serum. So, because of that I owe you my life." I grabbed her hand and pulled her closer. Staring deeply in her eyes I asked. "How can I ever repay you?"

Her cheeks flushed as she stared up at me. "Well," she started to say but was cut off by Kaden walking up.

"Hey bro, are you ready to hit the road?" He asked with a big kool-aid smile. I looked back at Alana and her facial expression had dulled.

"I guess you'll have to repay me through cashapp or something." She said in a slightly disappointed tone before turning and walking off towards her brother. I watched her walking away and realized I wasn't ready for our story to end. I turned back to Kaden and he was no longer smiling. I could tell by his facial expression that he had already read my mind.

"You ain't coming back are you?" He said in a partially crushed tone.

"Naw man, I don't think I am." I paused as my eyes traveled back to Alana. I couldn't help but watch her, as she stood joking and laughing with her brother. She gave off such a warm aura and being around her was such a comfort. Being around her had always given me a familiar feeling; it was as if I had maybe known her in a past life.

"You know who she reminds me of...right?" Kaden asked as he leaned back against the receptionist desk and matched his gaze with mine.

"Who," I said trying to look at him and watch her at the same time.

"Darlina." He said and then let out a small laugh.

"Man what?" I answered shockingly, but I knew he was right. I couldn't pinpoint it before, but now thinking of everything, she does remind me of Lina. She was chocolate, thick, smart and she made me laugh until my side hurts. She was the younger version of Lina. "Dude, you might be right."

"No, I am right." He answered and we both laughed again.

"Damn man, I didn't realize how much I missed you until right now." I said while shaking my head.

"Man, I know. That's why you need to come on back to the city. We need another epic summer." He added in a persuasive tone.

I looked at him and laughed. "Man, that summer involved Riley and Lina," I stressed. "We will never have a summer like that, and I just don't want to be put in that environment. It will be toxic for me. You know, I really loved Lina, but loving her was a bad habit, that I didn't need.

"How so?" Kaden asked with a raised brow.

"She was married, and I knew she was married, but I still pursued her. I went out that night not looking for love. You know what I mean?" I said giving him the look of a true player.

"Hell yeah, I know what you mean." He responded with a sly smile and I could tell he was catching my drift.

"And I definitely wasn't looking for a relationship. Hell, I already had enough women Falling for me like I was a Playboy. But it was something about Lina," I replied shaking my head again. My mind wandered around weighing the odds. "Man, that girl left me In my Feelings, and seeing them living the life we was supposed to have together…" My voice trailed off as visions of me and Lina played in my mind. "Man, that would leave me so Jaded." I said opening up my heart to him. "And you know I am going to have to be the one to play it nice."

"What do you mean, Nice for What?"

"Because I was in the wrong, I knew she was married but I pursued her. It will be best for me to just stay here and start over like I planned. You never know, maybe I can become the new deputy or something." I said loud enough for Duncan and everyone else to hear me.

"Alright, that's what I'm talking about." Duncan replied as him in the other two walked toward us. "Get with me later so we can work something out." He paused and looked me up and down.

"But you're definitely going to have to get your weight up." He joked and we all started to laugh.

"Ok...well...it's getting late." Kaden said while looking down at his phone. "I gotta get on the road." He continued and headed for the door.

"Hey, do you think I can catch a ride down there with you?" Scott asked out of the blue

"Yeah, that's cool." Kaden replied and then looked at me. "Hey, what do you want me to do with your car?"

"You have my car?"

"Yeah, it's been parked in my garage. You know I wasn't going to let them tow it away." He replied with a smile.

"Ayye, my man. Ima meet you guys outside. Don't leave me." I said as I walked over to Alana.

"Ight man, but don't be all day." Kaden replied before walking outside with Scott.

"So," I started to say, but then looked over at Duncan.

"What?" He asked innocently. Alana cleared her throat as if to say, 'beat it bro.' "Oh...my bad." He said realizing he had become the third wheel. "Let me go find myself some business." He continued and then headed out of the door to catch up with the fellas.

"Now, where were we. Oh right, how can I ever repay you?" I asked, giving her a flirtatious smile.

Hmmm…" she started as we walked towards the doors. "I guess we will talk about that when you get back." She said with a wink before pushing open the door and heading towards the guys.

I watched her for a second, my eyes traveling the curvature of her backside as she swayed away. I let out a breath of air and then followed out behind her. We all said our final good-byes and headed our separate ways. "Hey Kaden, let me drive man." I said and he tossed me the keys.

"Do you remember how to do it?" He joked as he got in the passenger seat.

"Real funny." I said while closing the door. "So," I said while starting up the engine. "Should we go up the hill or take the long way around?"

We all shot glances at each other.

"The long way." They said in unison before letting out a good laugh.

"The long way it is." I replied, pulling out of the parking lot and heading down the road. I glanced in the rearview mirror and felt a hint of relief as I watched the Hill House fade away in the distance.

The End

Made in the USA
Columbia, SC
16 November 2022

71360415R00120